BATTLE OF THE PSIONICS

Suddenly two huge arms wrapped around Chuck from behind. He felt a holstered gun the other man was wearing. But his arms were pinned too tightly.

Chuck reached out with his mind to pull the gun from the holster. Nothing happened.

It was as if his mind power had been shut down. Chuck gasped, straining more than he ever had, and still the gun would not come free.

"My God," a voice gasped from the darkness, "you've got one hell of a power, haven't you?"

PSI-MAN #2
Deathscape

Books in the PSI-MAN Series

PSI-MAN
DEATHSCAPE

MAIN STREET D.O.A.
(coming in April)

PSI-MAN

DEATHSCAPE

DAVID PETERS

DIAMOND BOOKS, NEW YORK

DEATHSCAPE

A Diamond Book/published by arrangement with
the author

PRINTING HISTORY
Diamond edition/January 1991

ISBN: 1-55773-450-X

Diamond Books are published by The Berkley Publishing
Group, 200 Madison Avenue, New York, New York 10016. The
name "DIAMOND" and its logo are trademarks
belonging to Charter Communications, Inc.

PRINTED IN THE UNITED STATES OF AMERICA

10 9 8 7 6 5 4 3 2 1

November 1, 2021

Thru

November 2, 2021

1

MOST CARS THAT came and went from the large building known throughout Boulder, Colorado, as the Internet Propulsion Laboratory used the single main road that ran to and from it. There were small connecting roads off to the side, but they led to high mountainous areas. No one lived there. People lived in town, or in the suburbs, but the idea of residing up in the mountainous regions? It was absurd.

As noted, no one lived there.

But hiding out there . . . that was something else again.

Up one of the steepest, most mountainous of roads drove the van. The sky was overcast and gray, much as it had been the day before and the day before that, and probably the way that it would be in all the succeeding days. The sun was setting, although the only way to tell was that the gray was simply becoming darker gray. There were stories of how, decades earlier, it was possible to sit on a cliffside and watch a great, glowing orb drop below the horizon line, the daylight being given over to night, stars appearing in the night sky. Just stories, though. Fantasies that many living in present days could not even remember.

The van was carefully neutral and nondescript. At the moment it was painted gray. Two weeks ago it had been blue, and eight weeks before that, white. Rattling around in the rear of the cargo bay was a small pile of license plates for easy conversion. It rolled up the incline on tires that were rapidly becoming threadbare, coughing in protest as gears shifted to urge it the rest of the way up the hill.

The van suddenly made a sharp right turn into a small pathway that no one would have been able to spot if they hadn't already known it was there. It swayed from side to side, the rattling becoming even more pronounced, and the man who was riding in the rear of the cargo bay held on with grim determination, uncomplaining, perhaps even resigned to his difficult lot in life. Nevertheless, he grunted slightly as if to register token protest.

The driver heard it and took immediate umbrage. "I'm doing the best I can, dammit," he snarled. There was no passenger seat next to him. They had ripped it out to provide as much room as possible.

"I know you are, goddammit, just drive," snapped the passenger. "Jesus, Buzz, get your head out of your butt, okay?" His legendary patience was starting to wear thin, and because of the abruptness and harshness of his reply, it startled the driver into silence.

The van made a final turn into a final, hard-to-see turnoff, and chugged through the darkness toward a ramshackle building. An angry barking sounded from up ahead in response to the rattlng of the van, but stopped as the van pulled up and the two men got out.

The driver, Buzz, clapped his hands together briskly, summoning the dog that he had raised from a pup. He remembered when he'd first seen Mars and judged by the paws that the dog was going to be large, even for a Doberman. Just how large he could not have imagined as Mars loomed out of the darkness, pausing slightly to confirm with scent what ears had already told him.

Mars lumbered forward, the blackness of his fur enabling him to blend with the night. If he remained still, he would merge with the shadows and no one would know he was there until he chose to make his presence known—a move that was usually fatal for the unwary.

Buzz rubbed on the back of the Dobie's huge neck, and the dog flattened out his ears. "Good to see you're keeping an eye on things," said Buzz, and then walked toward the house.

His strides were long, since Buzz was well over six feet tall. He wore faded jeans with holes in the knees, and an old army surplus jacket. His brown hair was long and straight, hanging down to around his shoulders but thinning on the top, and his thick moustache was uneven and needed a trim. His eyes were mostly hidden beneath his bushy eyebrows.

Buzz shoved open the door and was greeted by the sound of a hammer cocking in the darkness. He paused there and said dryly, "Someday, you asshole, you're going to blow me to kingdom come before I can open my mouth."

"That'd be an improvement," came floating from the darkness.

"Where's Jupe?" was asked by the other voice, a female.

Buzz chucked a thumb. "Coming."

"How's it scope?"

"Fine, Shai," said Buzz, glancing around. "Can't we have any goddamn light in here?"

"No. Somebody might see us."

"Like who, a raccoon? Gimme a break?" He had put a cigarette in his mouth and was holding a lighter up, about to light it.

There was an angry hiss, like a snake spit, and the lighter was blasted out of Buzz's hand, shattering. The bullet smacked into the wall behind.

He stood there a moment, his mouth moving but no sound emerging. "Shai, you—you asshole!" he managed to get out finally.

"Filthy habit," came Shai's voice.

"You could've killed me!"

"There's that. There's always that. Course if I wanted to kill you, you'd have a bullet in your brain right now."

There was a soft footfall behind Buzz, and he turned to see Jupiter standing in the doorway.

Jupiter had been the passenger in the van. He should have been right behind Buzz, but as always, he took his own sweet time getting anywhere. Privately, Buzz figured that it was because Jupiter was allowing for the possibility of a trap at all times, and figured that it would be preferable for Buzz to spring it.

Jupiter was a small man, especially in comparison to Buzz, and yet there was something about him that indisputably marked him as the leader. His body was lean and muscular, his neck long, and his face foxlike. His hair was close-cropped and blond, almost white. He surveyed the group, those he could see and those he couldn't.

Buzz pointed into the darkness. "Shai shot my lighter," he complained.

"Filthy habit," said Jupiter.

This drew a low laugh from the darkness, and an angry grimace from Buzz.

There was a slow shifting of feet as someone rose in the darkness, and moments later a tall man stepped from the dark. The deep blackness of his skin had hidden him well in much the same way that the darkness enfolded the Doberman on guard outside. His head was shaved clean, but a thin beard ran along the edges of his lantern jaw. He was cradling a sleek I&L automatic with nightscope and silencer, his preferred hand weapon and the one that he had used moments ago to dissuade Buzz from lighting up. In his deep voice he rumbled, "Buzz said it scopes. Buzz is an asshole, though. What you say, Jupe?"

"It scopes," agreed Jupiter in that smooth way he had. "In fact . . . we do it tonight."

"Aw, man," came the female voice, and now she stepped out as well into the pale light that the night sky was providing. "We do it tonight, by morning they'll be combing the area for us."

"No, Luta," replied Jupiter. "They will think we've fled the area. It won't occur to them that we'd be less than two miles away."

Luta pursed her lips. She looked small and withdrawn, habitually wearing clothes that were much too large on her. Her sleeves usually covered over her hands. Her red hair was close-cropped and hidden beneath a kerchief, her body equally hidden beneath the many layers of clothing. Her eyes were large and smoldering. "Bullshit," she said.

"It's not bullshit," replied Jupiter, but Luta wasn't listening anymore. She had retreated back into the darkness, there to murmur to herself and occasionally snarl angrily.

"You think we can take it?" said Shai after a moment.

"Yeah, we can take it," replied Jupiter.

"Place is guarded."

"No big deal. It's a quick in and out. We go in, we plant the bomb, we're out. One less place for our beloved government to be manufacturing poison."

"You sure?" said Shai. "Maybe it's a trap."

"It's no trap," said Jupiter. He leaned against a wall, his arms folded. "Remember, they think we're in Minnesota."

"We're not the only game in town, man," said Buzz. He automatically reached for a cigarette, then remembered that the trigger-happy Shai had dispatched his lighter. "Other groups are around, y'know. Scattered throughout the country. Get with the times, man. This is the twenty-first century, after all. We're not the only ones fighting for the environment."

"Maybe," agreed Jupiter, "but we're dropping, man. You hear about Porky?"

The others reacted with surprise, including Buzz who had been with Jupiter most of the day. Jupiter hadn't breathed a word about it. "What about Porky?" he said.

"Nailed him."

"No." Shai didn't want to believe it, and in the corner of the room, Luta gasped. "Shit no. Porky's a fucking legend, man."

"Yeah, well, now that's all he is," said Jupiter. "He and his people were in Chicago, and the Complex helped nail him."

"Aw, man." Shai was shaking his head and he walked the length of the room, blending in with the shadows. "Between the army and the Complex—man, whatever happened to government of the people and all that shit?"

"Somebody realized just how much shit it was," said Jupiter. "We gotta do this one, people. Do it big. Between the stuff they're producing in that factory and the waste material they produce making the stuff . . ."

"We got it," said Buzz, and shook his head. He shivered slightly. "Man . . . Porky. Can't believe it."

"Believe it," said Jupiter. "And believe that if we're not careful, we'll be next."

The comment hung there in the air, unresponded to. No one bothered to point out the obvious—that perhaps now would be the time for the group to split up. To give up the fight, to count as blessings that they had gotten away with as much as they did and be satisfied with that.

It was not suggested because it was not an option.

2

"CHUCK, THERE WAS nothing we could have done."

Dakota was saying the same thing for what seemed the hundredth time. And, as before, Chuck did not seem to be paying attention, or at least he didn't seem to believe it. Instead he just sat there opposite her at the table in the diner, rapping his knuckles in irritation on the stained tabletop.

Dakota shook her head as she studied him. His hair and beard were dark, and she knew by this point that although the beard was that natural color, the hair most certainly was not. The beard helped hide a jaw so square you could slice a pizza with it, and the fake color in his hair hid the blondness. He had a high forehead that made it seem to Dakota as if he had a great deal on his mind, which—if you counted knowing that you were a hunted man by a forbidding government agency (not to mention the fact that you were potentially the most powerful telekinetic on earth)—could certainly be counted as a great deal.

The gaze of his blue eyes hugged the tabletop. He had eaten his side order of spaghetti, leaving his entire veal cutlet over. He hadn't been in much of a mood to eat, and Dakota really couldn't blame him. Still . . . he had to snap out of it.

"Chuck, you hear me?" she said. "Earth to Chuck Simon."

He glanced up at her. "Don't use my name in public," he whispered.

"Finally something that got a response out of you," she said with a small measure of satisfaction. "Did you hear any of the other words I said?"

"I heard them. I just—"

"Just hated to hear them."

He shrugged his broad shoulders.

They were in a run-down diner in a run-down section of town. Boulder, like most cities since the start of the twenty-first century, had skidded downhill. The well-to-do lived far out in large palatial estates with guards and monitors or, even more popular these days, in underground cooperatives that were exclusive and pricey. The "tunnelers" were people who were convinced that nuclear holocaust was not too far off, and the cooperatives were designed for survival of that unfortunate (but probably inevitable) time. The best known was First Strike Estates, a virtual town unto itself where Mayor H. H. Hunter held sway, and any intruders were shot on sight.

But the poor and the not-so-well-to-do only had the cities in which to take refuge. Boulder was one such. Once a nice college town, albeit with a major drug problem. Now drugs were not a problem—at least, sales weren't. Money never changed hands, because of the Cards. Instead, everything was done with barter. Snap was the drug of choice, and Snap could get you anything—food, vehicles, sex—anything.

Chuck Simon was not interested in Snap.

He was interested, rather, in the vehicle they discovered quite by accident off by the side of the road when they approached Boulder. They got out when Rommel announced to Chuck, rather forcefully, that they better pull over or otherwise Rommel was going to take a dump in the back of the rickety pickup truck that served as their transportation. Taking the large German shepherd at his word, they indeed pulled over, and while Rommel was going about his business, he picked up the scent of the vehicle.

What a mess the thing was when they discovered it. A twisted heap of metal, the smell of alcohol permeating it. That the driver was drunk was beyond question. It was fortunate that he didn't take anyone with him when he dispatched himself.

However, he didn't, Chuck felt, deserve the fate he got. Chuck pried the door open, with a generous additional push from his mind, and found the poor bastard with his neck broken, the inflatable cushion in the steering column only partially inflated. Hell of a time for the safety bag to malfunction. Who knew how long he had been dead.

Get his wallet, Rommel said.

Chuck looked at his companion in surprise. "His wallet?"

"Good idea," Dakota said.

"I can't do that," Chuck said firmly. "It's wrong."

"Wrong to take his wallet? Why? He's not going to need it," Dakota pointed out matter-of-factly. "Besides, it was your idea."

"No it wasn't. It was Rommel's."

She glanced at the German shepherd, who stared back at her blandly. "Of course," she said tonelessly. "Foolish of me. Why should I think that a good idea came from you, Chuck? All right. Turn away so you don't have to watch."

"I can't," was the simple reply. But Chuck knew that she was right. The driver wasn't going to need it. And these days, you got your hand on a Card wherever and however you could. So he watched as Dakota rummaged through the corpse's pockets, pulled out his wallet, and moments later held up a plain white card with a little flourish.

Everyone had a Card. They were issued at birth, and had taken the place of money, of many important documents. More precisely, everyone had two Cards—the one they carried with them, and the original that was on permanent file with the Department of Identification, from which duplicates of lost, damaged, or stolen Cards could be obtained.

Chuck could not use his Card, of course. With the government tracking him, the last thing he wanted to do was leave a trail they could so easily trace. Instead he obtained black market fakes wherever he could, and on one occasion—a very early one—had swiped one from a soldier. But taking one off of a dead man . . . it gave him chills.

He sat in the diner now, feeling bleak and depressed. Dakota studied him for a moment and, believing there was an implied criticism of herself, said tightly, "What would you have preferred, huh? To waste an opportunity?"

He looked up at her and said, "As soon as we're out of Boulder, we contact the authorities and tell them about the dead man."

She blew air out from between her lips impatiently. "What's the point of that? It won't make him any less dead. And when they do find him, they close off his file and the Card becomes inactive. We're wasting an opportunity. As long as we keep the purchases small, people don't even bother to verify the retina patterns. And when the government finds out the guy is a stiff, what are they going to do? Come to the cemetery for payment?"

"That's fraud," he said quietly. "Besides, how do you know they won't hound the stiff's next of kin? And that's another thing. Don't you think his family is entitled to know he's dead? They're probably worried sick."

It was frustrating for her. On the one hand it was Chuck's high sense of morality and diligence that she found attractive. On the other hand, it sure could be a pain in the ass sometimes. "All right," she sighed finally, "all right, already. As soon as we're out of Boulder. Okay?"

"Okay." He smiled thinly at that. "Thank you."

"Don't thank me. I must be nuts. I'm probably nuts just being here with you."

"I warned you that you shouldn't come with me," he told

her. He fiddled with the straw that was sticking out of his half-emptied glass of soda. "But you did what you felt like doing. You could've stayed with the circus. Maybe you should go back," he added with a sigh. "Dakota, this is—"

Where's my food?

The brisk and rather sharp question came into Chuck's mind from just outside the window next to them. He mentally scolded himself. "Sorry."

"Sorry what?" said Dakota.

"Not you. The—"

"The dog, right," Dakota finished for him. "Y'know, you say you and that horse-sized dog of yours talk telepathically. Part of me thinks you're just jerking me around, but the other part—the majority, I guess—believes you."

"Why is that?"

"Because every so often you have these flashes of common sense, and I don't think they're coming from you."

"Uh-huh," said Chuck as he slid open the window next to him. Warm and heavy air washed over him as he tossed his untouched veal cutlet out the window. It never made it to the ground as Rommel, unseen below, caught it in his jaws.

That's it? came after a moment.

"That's it," said Chuck in a low voice, facing Dakota. She placed her chin at the base of her hand and watched the conversation with interest.

I'm still hungry. Get me a few steaks. Raw.

"It's bad enough I'm using a dead man's Card," murmured Chuck. "I don't have to destroy his credit rating, too."

That's another thing. There was all that meat in the car. You wouldn't let me eat it.

"What meat . . . oh," and Chuck felt faintly nauseated. "You mean the dead driver."

Yeah.

"That's disgusting."

"What is?" asked Dakota.

"Rommel is annoyed because I didn't let him eat the man in the car."

Dakota's face wrinkled as well.

A waste of perfectly good meat.

"Eating a dead human . . . it's awful, Rommel," Chuck whispered. "I'm picturing you doing it, and it makes me sick."

From below came the response, *You eat steak.*

"So?"

So what do you think a dead cow looks like? A bed of roses? You keep inflicting your morals on me, and my stomach keeps being empty.

"I thought you said you wouldn't eat humans anyway."

I said I wouldn't like to. They're stringy. But whatever is handy . . .

"Hold it," Chuck said nervously. "How do you know humans are stringy?"

"We are?" said Dakota, not exactly thrilled with the direction this conversation was taking. Her own recent meal was starting to turn in her stomach.

"How do you know?" Chuck demanded again.

There was silence at the other end.

"Rommel," he said warningly.

I've heard it around.

"You're lying."

Go neuter yourself.

Chuck was about to press the matter further when sharp footfalls next to him caused him to look up. And up.

Three very large individuals were standing next to him. Chuck knew their look and type immediately. Scruffy, unwashed, torn clothes, and a general air of insousciance, even anarchy about them. And these three, in addition, were extremely bulky, with large rolls of muscle hanging from their tattooed arms. They were known as "Cutters," and sometimes "Cardless Wonders."

Once upon a time, a more innocent time, Chuck would

have turned his nose up at them as if they were some lower form of life. They were blatantly disdainful of the government and of everything the government did that was supposedly in the best interests of the people. The government had taught all the good citizens, such as Chuck Simon, that Cutters were bad and the government good. And Chuck, like all the other good citizens, believed it.

That was before the government had dubbed Simon "Psi-Man," and put him at the top of their list of people they'd like to see either working as a government assassin, or otherwise simply dead. Neither option was, as far as Chuck was concerned, in his best interest.

Neither was picking a fight, which the Cutters for some reason seemed ready to do.

"Problem, friends?" asked Chuck slowly. "You want this table? We were just leaving."

Chuck started to get up from the table, gesturing to Dakota that she should do likewise.

The Cutter in the lead placed a firm hand on Chuck's shoulder and shoved him back down again.

You want me in there? came the terse question.

"I can handle it," Chuck muttered very, very softly.

Good. I'm so weak from lack of food anyway that I probably couldn't—

"Oh, shut up," Chuck said sharply.

The Cutter who had pushed Chuck down said slowly, thickly, with a gravelly voice, "You telling me to shut up?"

"He was talking to his dog," Dakota offered helpfully.

"Shut up, bitch," said the Cutter.

"Ooooookay."

"Gimme your Card," said the Cutter just behind him. "We feel like having dinner. And you're treating us."

The manager of the diner, who also happened to be the chef, stormed out from the kitchen. His bald head was glistening with sweat from standing over the grill, and his dirty smock was stretched over his ample stomach. "You guys are in here again!" he snarled.

"We like it here. Service is good," said the first Cutter.

Chuck glanced at Dakota and shrugged. "It's not worth fighting over," said Chuck, and he pulled the Card out of his shirt pocket. He handed it over to the Cutter.

"Thanks, man," said the Cutter.

The restaurant manager shouted angrily, "I'm calling the cops!"

"You do that," said the Cutter as Chuck rose quickly. Dakota did likewise and the two of them slid out from the booth to make way for the Cutters.

Except the Cutter who had, up until that moment, been silent reached out and grabbed Dakota by the shoulder. "She stays."

"Let go of me," said Dakota angrily.

Chuck hesitated only a moment. He had no desire to perform any unusual act, anything that could be described later to authorities as possibly paranormal in origin. Nevertheless, his reaction was largely automatic and instinctive.

"Let the lady go," Chuck told him.

Immediately the Cutter's hand flew away from Dakota's shoulder as if charged with reverse polarity. He stared at it in amazement, unsure of what had just happened.

Chuck did not want to give him the time to figure it out. "Let's go," he said quickly, and started for the door.

Not fast enough. The Cutter who had grabbed Dakota now came at Chuck from behind. Chuck started to turn but the Cutter was fast, faster than Chuck would have expected. He hurled himself against Chuck, his hands reaching around and grabbing Chuck by the wrists and pulling the smaller man's hands around behind his back.

Chuck grunted, staggered slightly, and said, "I wouldn't if I were you. I really don't want to hurt you."

The Cutter breathed hot, foul-smelling breath into Chuck's face as he said, "Oh, good. I was worried."

There was a roar from outside as Rommel instinctively tapped into the stress of the situation. The Cutters paused, confused and uncertain, and one of them said nervously, "What the fuck was that?"

At that moment, Chuck bent his knees, and put his left foot in front of his right. Quickly he brought his right arm up, the Cutter's automatically following. The Cutter hesitated, confused, thinking that Chuck was simply writhing in his grasp. Instead Chuck suddenly twisted his body and the Cutter staggered to the side, his right foot leaving the ground, totally off balance. Chuck spun his body and the Cutter left his feet altogether, the ground suddenly pinwheeling out from under him and then abruptly returning with force as the Cutter tumbled forward.

In a classroom where tomiki aikido was taught, or in a competition, the Cutter would have been able to go into a forward roll and recover quickly. In this situation though, the Cutter crashed to the floor. His neck and shoulders took the brunt of the impact and he screamed, pain shooting through him.

The other two Cutters hesitated only a moment and then came at Chuck.

Dakota leaped back into the booth, crouching, shielding herself. The closer of the two Cutters lunged for Chuck and swung a roundhouse at him. Chuck deflected the force of the blow, got the wrist and twisted quickly, pivoting. He twisted the Cutter's arm back, spun 180 degrees, pushed with one hand while pulling with the other.

He had misjudged his opponent's weight, though—the Cutter was big but surprisingly light. Chuck used too much force. The result was that the arm twist and follow-through hurled the Cutter onto the table and the man kept on going, smashing head-first through the window and falling to the ground outside.

Chuck heard a joyous bark and howl from outside, followed by a scream.

"NO!" shouted Chuck. "Rommel, no!"

The force of the dog's fury almost overwhelmed him. *Get out of my head!* snarled Rommel.

"Don't kill him!" Chuck commanded.

Chuck started toward the window, already able to envision the horrified Cutter lying helpless on the ground, Rommel's massive paws against his chest.

Dakota's shout alerted him a moment too late as a meathook-sized hand slammed down on the back of Chuck's neck. Chuck staggered forward, bracing himself on the edge of the table, his head swimming slightly. He started to reach out with his mind, to mentally hurl the attacker away even though he didn't want to display his power.

A plate sailed through the air, hurled like a Frisbee by Dakota's strong arm. It smashed into the Cutter's head and ricocheted away, and the Cutter staggered. Without looking Chuck lashed out with his leg, catching the Cutter just below the knees and sending him to the floor.

From outside came the sounds of ripping.

"Rommel, stop!" shouted Chuck as he ran for the door of the diner. Dakota followed him, stepping over the semiconscious forms of the Cutters and pausing only briefly, to grab the white Card that they had taken.

Chuck ran out to the front of the diner and screamed again, putting all the force of his mind behind it, "Back off, Rommel!"

There were people all around, poor people and people down on their luck, and none of them were doing anything to try and help the man who was being viciously mauled by the bloodthirsty canine. In a way, Dakota could understand it. If he stood on his hind legs, Rommel was probably the tallest individual on the block. As he was now, hunched over the Cutter, his jaws tinged red and his black eyes glowering, the curious "Z" in his fur, he looked like an animal you wouldn't want to get within miles of unless you were heavily armored.

Rommel had frozen on Chuck's command and now he stood there, unmoving, his entire body trembling in silent rage. Chuck approached him, step by step, not wanting to do anything that could possibly dislodge his very tenuous control. It was taking everything he had to override Rommel's primal blood lust.

"Back . . . off . . . Rommel," he said.

Why? There was unbridled fury in the transmission.

"Because I said so."

Who made you boss?

"God," said Chuck.

This stopped Rommel a moment. *Who's God?*

"He made everything."

Food?

"Yes, food. And the water you drink, and the air you breathe, and the bitches you hump. And he gave man dominion over all the animals."

Really.

"Yes, really."

I'll bet the animals weren't consulted about that decision.

Chuck had made it all the way to Rommel and now he reached down and pushed Rommel's quivering jaws away from the victim on the ground. "You're probably right," he said softly.

He turned and looked at the Cutter, a quick, superficial glance. The Cutter was moaning, and there were long, angry-looking rips and scars on his upper torso, and a long one down the side of his face. Nothing he wouldn't recover from, though.

Chuck turned quickly to the people who were standing around, the people who had been watching this odd man holding a conversation with no one that they could see. "Call an ambulance," he said.

No one moved.

"Somebody call an ambulance!" he repeated.

One man standing nearby, a young man with an arrogant manner, said, "Big deal, man, it's only a Cutter."

Chuck turned toward the man who had spoken and his control slipped just a bit as he snapped, "I don't care, call one!" and as he said it, his mind pushed ever so slightly, and the man staggered, pushed by an invisible fist. He was unsure what had caused it, but something suddenly warned him that it might be a good idea to do as this angry man (who talked to midair) had instructed.

Someone was tugging on Chuck's arm. He turned, tensing only a moment before relaxing upon seeing that it was Dakota. "What?" he said.

"Let's get to the truck," she said urgently. "Let's get out of here."

"We have to wait for the ambulance."

"But—"

"No buts," he cut her off. "I have to make sure he gets off all right. I can't just turn away."

She sighed, knowing better than to argue with him when he was like this. Impatiently she turned and headed off for the parking lot where the pickup was parked.

I'm hungry.

Without glancing at Rommel he grunted in a low voice, "Not now."

Dakota stalked across the small parking lot at the side of the building and climbed into the driver's side. She sat there, arms crossed, steaming.

What was the guy's problem, anyway? Why did he go around caring about other people so much? Couldn't he see that that sort of attitude was just going to get him into trouble? Was just going to get in the way?

Damn him anyway. It was infuriating. Chuck Simon was totally unreasonable. He had no sense of priority at all.

Except . . . it sort of depended on how one defined priority. For Dakota, her top priority was personal welfare: hers and his. For Chuck, top priority was . . . what? The welfare of all mankind?

She chewed on her lower lip, shaking her head. What was it that Chuck said he was? A Quaker? What the hell was a Quaker, anyway? All she knew was that she'd never met one, and if Chuck was indeed one, then the one Quaker she knew was pretty damned—

—concerned. Damn, but it was one of the things she found attractive about him; that he was a concerned, caring person. Except she didn't like it when it was inconvenient to her. But what did she expect him to do? Turn his nature on and off like a spigot? Now who was being unreasonable?

She glanced at her sideview mirror, sighing, and then sat upright, snapping from her slump. In the mirror was one of the Cutters, the one that Chuck had hurled to the floor.

He was walking away, though, quickly, glancing over his shoulder in her direction. Was he concerned that he'd been spotted? What was happening?

She reached for the door handle to get out, to go after him and demand to know what he wanted. Then she reconsidered, her hand moving away from the handle and settling in her lap. It was obvious what had happened. He'd seen her climb into the truck, had started to go after her, and then thought better of it. He had thought about his buddy, lying on the ground bleeding, and he had thought about Chuck tossing people around and Rommel chewing people up. He'd decided that these were not people he wanted to contend with.

She settled back and smiled. That was very wise of him, she decided.

The Cutter left the parking lot, glancing over his shoulder one more time. She hadn't spotted him. Great.

His hand was in his pocket, clutching the needle-sharp ice

pick. The ice pick he'd shoved into the right rear tire of the pickup truck that would cause a steady, slow leak. He hoped it would leave them stuck somewhere nice and inconvenient.

It wasn't much in the way of retribution, but it was all he had to offer. One had to get it where one could.

3

SERGEANT MARY JO Sanderson lay on her back, staring up at the sky and trying to recall the last time she had seen stars. At least, seen stars in the sky rather than as a result of her last serious drinking bout.

She heard a crack of thunder overhead, and from around her in the darkness came mutters of "Shit." "Knock it off," she said briskly. "That's why God invented tents."

The unhappy murmuring ceased, and Jo shook her head as she crawled into her own tent from which a soft light was emanating. Once inside she removed her helmet, running her fingers through her closely cropped blond hair.

She smiled ruefully. She remembered how, when she'd been drafted, she'd had hair so long it hung down to her ass. The day she had gone in for her regulation haircut, it had taken everything she could not to burst into tears as she saw huge clumps of hair littering the floor around her. The pile had resulted in awed murmurs of "Holy shit" from all around her, and she'd come to think of that moment as her first combat experience. She had been certain at that moment that nothing the army could throw at her subsequently would be anywhere near as devastating.

To a certain degree, she had been right. She had seen combat, intense enough that she had been decorated three times. But nothing had been quite as traumatic as that first encounter

with the rules and regulations that had, at one time, been the
enemy, but had since become her salvation and protector. She
had embraced that which could have destroyed her, and it
had made her strong.

She held her book up to the dim glow of the light and
began to read. From the darkness around her she heard scuf-
flings as the rest of her squad retreated to their tents. It was
good for them, she decided, these occasional night outings
on which she took her squad. The barracks at nearby Ft.
Morris were all too comfortable. Here, in the wilds of the
woods of Colorado, there was more of the spirit of adventure
that epitomized, to her, what the army was all about.

A soft rain began to fall, pattering against the tent, and
slowly it became a harder rain. Overhead the sky rumbled
more and more loudly, lit up and danced to the tune being
fiddled by the electric bows of lightning. Jo huddled closer
to the light to see better. Technically she should have called
for lights out considering the time, but all things considered
she didn't see much harm in turning a blind eye to it and
letting the men keep the lights on for as long as they wished.
It's not as if they were providing targets for passing bombers.

Embrace the rules, sure, but don't strangle to death in their
grip.

She wasn't sure what time she had drifted off. All she knew
was that she was brought to startled wakefulness by the explosion. The massive, rolling explosion that reverberated
through the woods and roused everyone around her in the
darkness with shouts and profanities. Not just an explosion,
but a series, one feeding off the other. As one faded, another
followed it up, becoming louder as if a giant were moving
toward them with massive, echoing steps.

"What the hell is that?!" came from nearby.

She had no answer, but she knew what was situated in the
direction of the explosion, and she didn't like the conclusion
she was drawing. Jo ran out of her tent, pulling on her helmet

and shouting orders for her squad to assemble. The rain was still coming down, her boots squishing in the mud around them. Something was going down, something big. All of a sudden, Sergeant Jo Sanderson's squad had genuine night maneuvers on their hands.

And that was when she heard the scream. It was deafening, smashing through her head, and she staggered under the pure buffeting force of it. She fell to the ground, her face in the mud, and writhed in the pain of it. Someone pulled her to her feet, she wasn't sure who, and someone— Private Dorsch, she thought—was shouting in her face, his expression one of concern. But she didn't understand what he was saying, didn't understand anything except the intensity of the pain and agony that was lancing through her as if someone were taking a screwdriver and a ballpeen hammer and slamming the screwdriver through her head and out the other side. Instinctively, having no idea why, she clutched at her eyes.

Her legs had lost their strength and she sagged in the soldier's grip. *My God, I'm dying,* she thought, and then, even worse, *My God, I'm frightened.* Yes, far worse. Dying was easy. Living with the concept that a frightening situation can overwhelm one, though—that was a concept she could not begin to deal with.

Sound came back to her by degrees, as if someone were slowly adjusting upward the volume on her mental television set. "Sergeant!" came the shouted voice of concern from Dorsch, and now others were gathering around him.

It was dark, they couldn't see her face. They wouldn't see the fear and panic, the confusion in it as she came to the slow realization that something very wrong had happened. That something, somehow, had entered her mind from the outside. That her thoughts were not her own.

She was peering out at them from between mud-covered fingers. Slowly Jo lowered her hands, composing herself, trying to situate her mental attitude so that when she did speak, it would be in a confident, determined voice instead of one filled with the confusion and panic she felt.

"Pack up the gear. We're moving out. Let's find out what the hell that was," she said tautly.

4

"THAT'S JUST GREAT."

The light drizzle had just begun to fall as Chuck stood toward the back of the truck, staring at the flat tire. He kicked it reprovingly, as if that might stir it back to life.

It was bad enough that they had taken a wrong turn en route to the highway and were now on this large road that seemed to be going nowhere they wanted to go. But now this, standing on this side of a road in the middle of nowhere . . .

Although, curiously, there were halogen lamps mounted every few yards. Obviously this was a well-traveled road, nowhere or not, and someone had gone out of their way to make sure that it was easy to see.

What was even easier to see was that they were in serious trouble. Rommel, in the back of the pickup truck, was resting on his forepaws and looking at Chuck with boredom.

Do something, he told him.

Chuck glanced at Rommel. "I could always ride you," he said.

Never happen.

"You're right. I'd need a saddle." He turned toward Dakota who was still in the cab. His hair was already slicked down from the rain, which was starting to come down a bit harder. "Where's the spare?" he called out, kicking the flat again.

"You just kicked it," she replied.

He looked back at the flat tire. "Great. Just great."

He trotted up to the cab and Dakota rolled down the window. "I think I see lights up ahead," he said, pointing east. "Maybe someone up there can help us out. You stay here."

"No argument. You taking Rommel?"

He and Rommel exchanged glances. Rommel looked distinctly uninterested in setting out on a trek along the roadside.

Gee, if only he did have a saddle.

"Rommel, you stay here," said Chuck.

I stay with you.

Chuck felt touched by the loyalty. "Look, I know you want to protect me . . ."

The hell with that. You're the one who feeds me. If you leave, I don't get fed.

He sighed. "Man's best friend."

Where? Rommel looked around.

"Look, I really want you to stay with Dakota. I don't like the thought of her being stuck by the roadside at night all alone. I want you to protect her."

From wild animals?

"From people."

Same thing.

"True. Very true. So you'll stay with her."

There was a pause, which was unusual. Rommel typically responded within moments. His thought process was endlessly fascinating to Chuck: clear, straightforward, concerned with a dazzling paucity of things and how they related to his life. The rest, from sentiment to theology, was generally brushed off as irrelevant.

I'll stay with her.

"Thank you," said Chuck with a sigh of relief.

Be careful.

"Why? Because if something happens to me, you won't get fed?"

That too.

"Too?" said Chuck with a rueful laugh. "What else is there?"

Just be careful, you stupid human.

Chuck was touched. But somehow he had the feeling he shouldn't say anything. It might spoil the moment. Besides which, the rain was coming down a bit harder now. He pulled the top of his jacket up over his head to give him some measure of shelter and started off at a slow run up the road.

If he had been alone, or if it were just Rommel and himself, he might have just battened down the hatches and waited in the truck for the rain to pass. But there was Dakota to consider—he didn't like having to be stuck with her in the middle of nowhere, especially since one never knew what might come along. Also, after these months on the run, he had lost the ability to feel comfortable in one place. He had to keep moving, always moving, afraid that someone might be on his heels at any moment. Which they probably were.

Dakota turned in her seat and looked out the back window. Rommel was sitting in the rear of the truck, looking wet and somewhat annoyed.

Her lips twitched in sympathy. She reached over and opened the door on the passenger side and gestured for Rommel to climb down from the back and up into the cab. Rommel, for his part, merely stared at her as if she had lost her mind.

Impatiently she waved again, thinking, *This is the genius dog Chuck talks to all the time? Christ.* This time, Rommel seemed to get it, or at least deigned to pay attention to it. Moments later he was squeezing his considerable hulk into the cab next to Dakota, and it was at that point she wondered if this indeed had been such a keen idea after all. As Rommel climbed in he seemed to just keep coming and coming as if he were endless. His muzzle was pressed against the windshield, his haunches were shoved down against the seat, and he couldn't seem to find anywhere comfortable to place his paws.

Rain was coming down harder and Dakota tried to reach across to pull the door shut. It was with some frustration that she discovered that she could not, because now Rommel was blocking the way.

With a few choice words of disgust, she climbed down from the driver's side, walked around and, in so doing, getting herself good and soaked, got to the passenger side, slammed the door shut—

There was a howl of anger. She saw a few tufts of fur sticking out and realized to her horror that she'd caught Rommel's tail.

She yanked the door open and Rommel pulled it in, growling. She closed it again, this time far more gingerly. Then she walked back around to the other side and slowly climbed in. Rommel was glaring at her, a rumble in his throat like a tractor.

She forced a smile.

"You like show tunes?" she asked.

Chuck tried to stay to the side of the road. Originally he had been walking toward the middle, but when he had tried to flag down a large truck heading in the opposite direction, it had shot right past him without slowing down. It had not been very encouraging.

He didn't think the rain could come down harder, but it did. This trudging along was taking him absolutely forever. If only there were some way to hurry things along.

It was then that he hit upon an idea. Every time he had tried to use his TK to lift something heavier than he himself could carry, he had failed. That was why his power couldn't help him, for example, lift the truck and compensate for the blown tire. But he could benchpress his own weight.

Maybe he could fly.

He stood dead still and tried to concentrate on lifting himself up. He envisioned a giant fist reaching down, for it had helped him in the past to lift things by visualizing a hand doing so. He closed his eyes, spread out his arms, and pictured the hand lifting him high in the air.

When he opened his eyes and looked down, he hadn't budged a fraction of an inch.

Maybe, he decided, it was like sitting in a chair and trying to lift the chair while you were in it. Two forces working against each other. Or maybe it was his mild fear of heights that was somehow short-circuiting his power, preventing it from placing him into a difficult and potentially phobic situation. Or maybe he was just stupid.

Still, it occurred to him that perhaps, at least, he could give himself a boost. He started to run, mentally picking a point at which he would leap, and the moment he hit it, he mentally shoved away at the ground.

He sailed through the air in a dazzling, thirty-foot broad jump, and was just congratulating himself when he started to come down again. He hit the ground and landed on his ass, skidding out of control for a good ten feet before tumbling off the road and into a ditch. He lay there for a minute or so, getting back his breath and, in addition, getting covered with mud to go with his general look of sogginess.

Slowly he sat up, shaking off the feeling of being a drowned rat. All right. He couldn't fly. He couldn't leap long distances, much less a tall building in a single bound. At this rate he was never going to be a comic-book hero.

He got up and started to walk again on unsteady legs.

Within a few more minutes, he came within sight of what appeared to be a large gate to somewhere.

He hesitated. Perhaps it was a government installation, and he had no idea how thoroughly word had been spread about him. Would they recognize him on sight? Shoot, maybe?

Well, if they tried to shoot him, certainly his TK could protect him. But what if . . . ?

He shivered, becoming chilled to the bone. It started to
dawn on him that the old saying, "Any port in a storm,"
was an old saying because it still held true. He was in one
hell of a storm, and he was most definitely in need of a port.

Squinting to see as best he could through the rain, Chuck
started to run at a quick pace. As he got nearer, he saw a
large, lighted sign hanging on a fence just to the right of the
gate. It read *Internet Propulsion Laboratories*. Well, that
seemed harmless enough.

He got to within sight of the guard booth at the gate, which
he certainly hoped was manned at this time of night. The
huge gates were electronic, at least eight feet high, with sharp
and rusty points at the top.

He started to slow down for no reason he could finger. By
the time he was within a couple of feet of the gate he had
come to a stop.

Something was wrong.

Rommel stared listlessly at Dakota, who was trying desperately to keep up her end of the conversation.

"So the guy says to his dog, 'Who's your favorite baseball
player?' And the dog says, 'Rooth. Rooth.' Like a bark, see?
And the bartender says, 'Get outta here, that dog can't talk,'
and he throws the two of them out. And the dog looks up at
the guy and says," and she snickered slightly. " 'Ya think I
shoulda said DiMaggio?' "

She stared at Rommel, waiting for a response. Rommel
just stared back at her.

"Critic," she said.

Suddenly Rommel tensed. Dakota was a little startled by
the abrupt movement. It was as if electricity had suddenly
filled the cab.

"What is it?" said Dakota softly. "What is it, boy? Is
something wrong?" When there was no reply, she said, "Is

it Timmy? Is he trapped in a barn?'' She had no idea what that meant, but her own mother had always said it when their family dog was acting strange, and her father had always laughed, and when she'd asked them to explain it they had said in that way they had, ''You wouldn't understand.'' Well, hell, she didn't understand now, either.

''It's Chuck, isn't it?'' she said.

Rommel looked at her as if responding to the spoken name. All this time, Dakota had been unsure of whether Chuck was really pulling her leg when he said he spoke to the dog. Or maybe he really believed it and was just a little nuts. Either way, she really wished at that moment that if Rommel could talk, could communicate at all, he would *say* something already.

Because she was starting to get very, very nervous.

Chuck put his hands against the bars and looked through the gate, peering at the guardhouse within and squinting. The light inside it was extinguished, and there wasn't enough illumination from an obscured moon to provide anything with which to see.

Except he was able to see enough. He was able to see a dark form slumped halfway out of the guardhouse.

Chuck shouted out, shouted for help, and rattled the gate. There was no response from the guardhouse or from anywhere nearby.

He stepped back, closing his eyes, focusing his power and his concentration. His breathing slowed, his muscles tensing at first and then relaxing as he forced a calm through himself. He reached into the core of himself and found the power there, found it strong and throbbing. He drew it up into his mind, readied it.

His eyes snapped open and his head twitched convulsively, as if he had just hurled something from his temple. The invisible power lashed out, cracking into the gate. The gate blew open with a loud crash and klang as the doors flew in opposite directions from each other, smacking into the fence.

Chuck paused, catching his breath, and then bolted through and to the guardhouse. He dropped to his knees, examined the corpse that was lying there . . .

No, not a corpse, for a low moan issued from it. The guard was in his late fifties, probably a retired cop, in a position that was secure behind its electronic gate and low exposure to risk. He rubbed a bruise that was swelling on the back of his bald head as Chuck said to him urgently, "What happened? Who did this?"

"Don't know," he gasped. "Extremists, I think . . ."

Chuck blanched. Extremists. For a moment, the good, government-trained citizen that he had been rose in indignation. Extremists were bad. Extremists were evil. Extremists disagreed with the policies of the government, disagreed with the wars that the government was fighting. Extremists made their displeasure known by blowing up factories where work was being done on weapons and such.

But that was the Chuck Simon of Ohio talking. The Psi-Man—the assassin on the run that the government was after—hell, he was considered worse than the worst of Extremists. Perhaps it was time to start reconsidering his opinions. Still . . .

"What is this place?" Chuck said.

"Internet . . . Propulsion Labs . . ." The guard was trying to sit up, and blood was trickling down his face. A cut had opened up on his forehead. "They pulled up . . . in a truck . . . had some gizmo that overroad the electronic lock . . ." His hand was fumbling for a phone. "Gotta call . . . help. . ."

His hand went to where the receiver was, but all he was greeted with was pieces of plastic. "Broke my phone . . ." he said, sounding more confused. Clearly he was concussed, not thinking properly.

"Where are they?"

"Went to lab . . . just a few minutes ago . . ."

"Anyone up there?"

"My daughter . . . my daughter . . ."

The guard said it another two times or so, and Chuck's mind was racing. Cut off from communication, and Extremists were in this lab. Chances were they were going to blow it up. And this poor man's daughter was there. Probably a technical worker, or maybe a custodial person. The Extremists might try to make sure the place was empty before they blew it . . . or they might not.

He couldn't turn away. Something had to be done, and police or soldiers would never arrive in time to do it.

". . . my daughter . . ."

"Leave it to me," said Chuck. "I'll save your daughter."

The rain was coming down harder, but he ignored it as he dashed out of the guard's house and ran up the path. This time he actually managed to give some extra kick to his strides by using his power to push off in small bursts. He made tremendous time.

Unfortunately, he made such good time that he wasn't there to hear the guard say, "My daughter . . . have to call my daughter in town . . . tell her what happened . . . thank God . . . the plant is empty . . ."

Rommel began to bark furiously. Dakota had never heard him bark quite like that, or at least not from that close up. She thought she was going to go deaf.

He leaped up and slammed his paws against the windshield. A crack ribboned across it.

"Jesus," shouted Dakota, "hold on!" She jumped out of the driver's seat, throwing open the door and alighting on the rain-slicked road. Rommel practically exploded from the car, hitting the ground and skidding slightly. Then the great dog caught himself, spun, and started to run at full speed in the direction that Chuck had gone.

Dakota stood there a moment, her hair becoming plastered

to her face, her clothes starting to soak through. She considered that perhaps just climbing back into the truck would be the best thing to do.

Then she pictured Chuck lying somewhere in a ditch, bleeding and dying. Unbidden she imagined an image of the body they had discovered, and the karmic concept that such a fate would come around to visit itself upon Chuck . . .

With a feeling that she was going to regret this decision, Dakota ran off after Rommel, who was already fading in the distance.

Chuck approached the front of the building cautiously, probing with his mind. There was trouble, a disturbance somewhere within the building. He could not localize, but he could definitely feel it.

The rain pelted him, and now the wind was howling. It was a long, mournful howl that put him in mind of Rommel. Right now he would like nothing better than to have that homicidal mastiff at his side, even if the creature did have a certain knack for ripping warm-blooded beings into bite-sized chunks. He couldn't even communicate with him, for they were out of range of Chuck's power. He had a vague feeling of Rommel, but that was all.

The front door slid open silently. He was going unchallenged, had penetrated this far into the labs. He didn't like it one bit.

Then he saw something he liked even less.

Halfway down the hall was a monibot—the squat, heavily armed and dangerous units that were used for routine hall patrol in many high-tech installations. As robots go they were pretty simple and, as was usual for robots, highly single-functional. They were unable to distinguish between friend or foe, which was why they were never going to replace soldiers. Monibots were armed with motion detectors and Rapidoshots, one eighty-round chamber mounted on either side. Basically, if anything larger than a mouse moved, it was perforated until it stopped moving.

It was impossible to shut them off in person. Their remote power flow came from a security system situated some miles away that provided service to many such devices throughout the area. The only way to dispose of them was for the guard to have contacted the security system on the phone, given them certain privileged information, and requested a shutdown while explaining the necessity. Without that, the only thing to do was wait until 8 A.M. the next business day when the monibots shut down automatically.

Whoever had penetrated the perimeter had done neither. The monibot was tilted on its side, its center panel blown out and lying a couple of feet away on the floor, twisted into scrap. Its electronic eyes were dark and lifeless, and the muzzles of the Rapidoshots hung impotently downward.

"What the devil—?" breathed Chuck.

With his TK he probably could have handled any monibots he came upon—probably still could, if he had to. But someone had come through and saved him the necessity.

He started to make his way through the shining steel corridors, glancing around nervously. His sneakered feet squeaked on the polished floor, and every so often he glanced at his own distorted reflection.

He wasn't quite certain where he was going. He was operating entirely on instinct, but his instinct had grown to be fairly reliable and he'd learned to trust it.

A right, another right, then a left, and he moved faster now. His mind was racing far ahead of him. If the guard's daughter was working late, how did she avoid being riddled with bullets by the monibots? Perhaps there were some security holes that he was unaware of—a code word, perhaps, or a localized shut-off device provided to key personnel.

What had blown out that robot? And now he passed another one—each was programmed to patrol its own quadrant, so they never overlapped and started shooting each other.

This robot, just like the first one, had been totaled. Not only that, but something had been scribbled on this one. He crouched down, squinting at the words, scrawled in what seemed a female hand, *Klaatu Barata Nikto*. He whispered the words to himself, confused as anything. What the hell was that phrase supposed to mean? Sounded like Latin a little, but he couldn't be sure. Foreign languages had never been his strength.

As he was studying the robot, the hair on the back of his head began to rise. It barely gave him warning before a low growl reached his ears.

The Doberman was standing there, snarling, maw drawn back exposing razor-sharp teeth. It was big, big enough to give Rommel a run for his money. But Rommel wasn't here. And Chuck was suddenly wishing that, wherever Rommel was, Chuck was with him.

The animal uttered one short, furious bark and then leaped at Chuck.

It slammed into Chuck, its teeth snapping at Chuck's face, but before it could press the momentary advantage, the shocked animal was being lifted off the ground by an invisible force. It kept going up, up until it slammed into the ceiling overhead and let out a confused and frightened yelp.

Chuck placed his hand against his chest, trying to recover his breath. He had a nasty scratch from the creature's claws, and in short order it would definitely start to sting like hell. For now, it served as a sharp reminder that Chuck couldn't let his guard down even for an instant. His momentary lapse in concentration had cost him. The dog shouldn't have slowed him down for a moment, Dobie or not. But Chuck had been startled, and that moment of confusion had been enough for the dog to score a hit.

Next time an opponent might not miss.

He slowly got to his feet and stared at the dog, madly running in midair, unable to find purchase on anything. Chuck smiled mirthlessly, taking no joy in the animal's plight.

"Psi-Man says go home, boy," he said.

In response the dog hurtled away down the corridor. For good measure, Chuck spun the dog like a pinwheel, the dog's body making brisk *whoop-whoop* noises as it sailed down the hallway. As soon as the dog was out of sight, Chuck released his mental hold and heard the dog thud to the ground. Chuck paused, waiting for the animal's renewed charge, but all he heard were the desperate sounds of retreat.

He realized then that the dog might lead him to whomever he was trying to find, and he started after it. But within moments he had become lost again in the maze of corridors and cross hallways.

He spun on his heel, trying to find a way out. Trying to sense which was the direction to go. But oddly, he wasn't feeling anything anymore. Whatever instinct had guided him was suddenly shut down, as if it had decided to go for a coffee break.

He glanced off to his right and saw a large, darkened conference room. There was a long table in it, with a tabletop made out of some sort of ebony material that seemed so dark that it might have absorbed all available light, like a black hole. Just past it was a huge bay window, opening out on what seemed to be a stunning view. Chuck had never seen anything quite like it, living in the relative obscurity and blandness of LeQuier, Ohio.

He approached it slowly, for a moment his mission forgotten. His senses were ensnared instead by the beauty of the view. The noise from his shoes that squeaked on the glistening hallway floor vanished as he entered the conference room, for the room was carpeted in rich, dark shag. He walked across and placed his palms against the window, his breath caught.

He hadn't realized that the back of the building faced onto a cliff. Far below the cliff, in what seemed an immeasurable distance, rolled the waters of some river. Even though it was night, he could see the telltale white bubbling that gave an indication of the speed with which the water was moving. The rain was still coming down hard.

"Beautiful, isn't it?"

He spun quickly, surprised and confused. He had not sensed anybody, not expected anybody. And yet here somebody was, a foxlike man, pale and unnerving, standing framed in the doorway, looking completely at ease.

"Stunning view," he said. "It was once unspoiled timberland, you know."

Chuck circled slowly, keeping the table between himself and the newcomer. "It looks pretty unspoiled to me."

"Yes, well, it would. That's because you don't know where to look. For example, that lovely river down there? Polluted." The smaller man was moving now and Chuck kept circling, the smaller man coming toward him. There was something about him that Chuck found very unnerving. The man spoke as he moved, slow and unhurried. "Polluted by the waste from experimental chemicals this place produces."

"What chemical waste?"

"Don't play stupid," said the man. "You work here. You know."

"I don't work here. I just came by because I saw there was trouble."

The smaller man laughed curtly at that. "Oh. Right. I suppose you hadn't heard: Good samaritans went out of style ages ago."

"Who are you?"

"We're here to blow up your bosses' plant."

"They're not my bosses, but you can't do that."

"Don't get cocky," said the smaller man, stabbing an impatient figure at Chuck. Chuck was still circling, and had practically gone all the way back around to the door. "You did something to Mars, I'll grant you that. Scared the doggie doo out of him. But us, we've been through too much. We don't scare."

"Neither do I," said Chuck, stopping and standing his ground.

As if taking his cue from Chuck, the smaller man stopped as well. "You would," he said sincerely. "You would if you knew what we know. The things the government hushes up, so that only the brass at the top, top levels knows. For example, did you know that the stuff they pump into the water is having a major ecological effect? Not just killing plants around the river, no. It's affecting the animal life. There're rumors going around about all sorts of creatures wandering the woods. Mutant deer and bears, stalking around, altered and driven berserk by the wastes from experimental drugs being pumped into the water by mankind. Creatures that hunters' bullets don't stop. That nothing short of a bazooka can stop. That's our contribution to the ecological balance. And you think we should be stopped from blowing this nightmare up? We should be given medals."

Chuck stared at him for a long moment. "I know," he said softly, "I know you believe in what you're saying. Christ, I don't know, maybe you're right. But I can't just stand here and let you blow this place up, for whatever reason. There are lives at stake—"

"Just yours, and you don't count," said the smaller man, and then with an odd inflection he added, "Shai."

Chuck didn't know what the man was talking about until suddenly two huge arms wrapped around him from behind. The bare arms of a massively muscled black man crisscrossed Chuck's chest, pain shooting through him as the hold massaged the fearsome cut he had sustained.

Dammit, he should have sensed him coming! What the hell was wrong with him?

"What should I do with him, Jupe?" The deep voice had a faint Jamaican lilt to it. Against his buttocks, Chuck felt a holstered gun the other man was wearing. But his arms were pinned too tightly . . .

Well, hell, why should that stop him?

Chuck reached out with his mind to pull the gun from the holster. He wouldn't fire it, of course. He would not kill, under any circumstances. But, despite the harsh words of this smaller fellow, a floating gun aimed down his throat should go a long way toward spooking him rather seriously.

Nothing happened. The gun would not move from his holster.

It was as if his mind power had been shut down. Chuck gasped, straining more than he ever had, even more than in the days when he was not yet fully conversant with his power and every movement was a difficulty. And still the gun would not come free.

The one called Jupe, however, was staggering as if struck. "My God," he gasped out, "you've got one hell of a power, haven't you?"

Shai looked from one to the other in confusion. "This little guy? He's got—"

Chuck didn't know what was happening, didn't care. All he knew was that his breathing was becoming more labored from the increasing pressure of the man behind him. He felt as if his rib cage were about to collapse. And whatever was happening to him, this was no time to form an overdependency on his TK power.

Even as all this raced through his mind, he slammed down on the instep of the man called Shai. Shai grunted in anger and annoyance, and Chuck managed to bring up his right hand enough to squirm it around and grab hold of Shai's wrist.

Chuck twisted it, hard, and like snapping a whip, Shai's entire body had to suddenly jerk around and contort to follow its path. Before Shai knew it, rather than being behind Chuck and squeezing, he was facing Chuck with his own wrist creaking under Chuck's grip.

Shai brought up his free hand, fingers curled, hard base of his hand as the driving impact point. It came around with blinding speed and Chuck blocked it, but just barely. The movement enabled Shai to shake loose, and the black man spun away and suddenly snapped into an alert defensive stance.

Chuck was standing several feet away, and immediately fell into a relaxed aikido defensive posture. He readied himself for Shai's attack. And Shai would attack, of that he had no doubt.

Aikido was a discipline with no offensive moves, only defensive. Chuck would only react rather than act. It was up to Shai to make the first move.

Shai did, coming in quickly, lashing out with a side snap kick. Chuck stepped aside, brushing past the leg, using its own speed against it, and flipping Shai across the room. Shai's back hit the table and he rolled across it, slamming into the far wall just under the window. The glass rattled with the impact.

Shai scrambled to his feet, growling angrily. And from across the room, off to the side, Jupe said in annoyance, "For God's sake, Shai. Shoot him."

Chuck froze, for the gun was now in Shai's hand like lightning. He tried with all his power to yank the gun away and still his mind betrayed him. But Jupe staggered, and he moaned, "I can't hold him forever!"

It was then that Chuck realized what was happening. Jupe—Jupiter, most likely—was negating his own psi power. He was overriding Chuck's psychic ability with one of his own. He looked from Jupiter to Shai and back, unsure of which one to deal with first.

"He's a worthy fighter," said Shai tautly, the gun never wavering from its aim on Chuck. "It's not fair to me to shoot him from here. He deserves to meet me hand-to-hand."

"Screw that!" snapped Jupiter. "Dammit, Shai, do what I'm telling you! Kill him!"

Shai flashed his white teeth that seemed to glow in the darkness against his face. "Sorry, man," he said.

He fired once.

Chuck pitched back, fingers flying for his head. Blood welled up from between his fingers and he hit the floor with a wet, sickly thud.

"Damn," Shai said softly. "Goddamn."

Jupiter let out a sigh as he felt the pressure ease. Then he tossed an angry look at Shai. "Since when do you question my orders?"

Shai was stonily silent. And Jupiter, slowly realizing what was at stake, said more softly, "I understand, Shai. Really. But we've got priorities. Buzz and Luta must almost be finished with the gizmo by now. We have to keep on schedule. Luta's blitzing the monibots was necessary, but it certainly alerted the central security HQ. They'll be sending people. So let's remember the job we have to do and do it, okay?"

This was met with a low grunt, and Jupiter took that as an affirmative. He ran out, Shai right behind him.

Chuck's body lay unmoving and there was no sound, save for the splattering of rain against the window.

5

THUNDER RUMBLED AND lightning split the sky overhead. Dakota staggered, even stumbled slightly, but a tightrope walker doesn't fall quite that easily.

Unless the tightrope walker hits a pothole filled with water. Which is what Dakota did, and she went down with a cry. She fell flat, trying to absorb the impact with her hands as best she could. But when she fell it was at a bad angle, and when she went down it was with her leg at a bad angle to her foot.

She banged her fist on the road in frustration, but she didn't realize at first the severity of her injury. She realized, though, when she tried to stand and pain lanced through her lower leg as if someone had slammed a javelin through. She cried out and fell again, this time banging her knee. But that was nothing compared to the throbbing that had seized hold of her calf.

She looked up and Rommel was nowhere in sight. There, in the distance, was what appeared to be a fence of some sort, a fence and a gate. And far beyond that, buildings. She even thought that in the distance she heard Rommel barking angrily.

Suddenly the gates far in front of her opened and a van roared out. Tires screeching, it turned sharply and roared down the road . . . straight at her.

Dakota shrieked, throwing up her arms to ward off the impact that she was certain she was about to feel . . . certain that her last thought was going to be, *What a stupid way to die.* She staggered, trying to get out of the van's way, but her ankle betrayed her and she fell for a third time, ripping up her palms on the road. Then all she could see were headlights, nothing but headlights flooding her field of vision.

She heard a shout, and then the van screamed to a halt, brakes catching and slowing the van so that it stopped mere inches in front of her. Dakota's heart pounded against her chest and she looked up in confusion as the door of the van opened and a tall man with dark hair—black, perhaps, or maybe brown—and a moustache leaped out of the van. He skidded slightly when he hit the ground and barely caught himself on the door handle.

"Christ, what are you doing here?" he shouted over the pounding rain.

"I'm looking for someone!" she shouted back. "Have you seen him?" She was trying to stagger to her feet, wincing. "Dressed kind of like me, with dark hair and beard . . . he was on up ahead of me . . ."

And now another man stepped out from the other side, a foxlike man. Whereas the first man seemed bothered by the rain and was muttering under his breath, this man barely noticed it.

She couldn't make out his eyes, for it seemed as if his face were cast in shadow. He stood there for a moment, seeming to size her up. "Was this man," he said slowly, "a rather skilled fighter . . . with psionic powers?"

She gasped, incredulous. Automatically, out of defensive habit, she wanted to deny it, to laugh off the suggestion that anyone, much less Chuck, would be possessed of powers of the mind. But this was not the situation to toss around bullshit, and she was getting the overwhelming feeling that this was definitely not the man to toss it at.

"Yes," she said after a moment's thought. "I . . . we work together."

"You did," he said.

His quiet, certain emphasis on the past tense startled her. "What are you talking about?"

That was when the explosion—the same one that Jo Sanderson was witness to—lit up the sky.

Rommel squeezed between the bars of the gate and started up the road. With the rain coming down as hard as it was, he stuck to the more tree-filled perimeter rather than running straight down the main road. It afforded him some measure, albeit small, of protection. It also enabled him to come nowhere near the van that was speeding down the main road toward the gate.

As a result, while Dakota was having her confrontation with the Extremists, Rommel was just approaching the main building.

He barked in agitation, because he sensed that something was wrong. Chuck needed him, needed him desperately. What had been even more alarming for Rommel was that, for a time, he had completely lost sense of Chuck. Even when Chuck wasn't around, Rommel *sensed* him deep within his mind. They couldn't communicate—Chuck generally had to be face-to-face to do that, although their range was improving all the time. But Rommel felt him, as deeply as his drive for food or self-protection. It had become a part of his psychological makeup, part of his instinct.

Except Chuck was gone, as if their tie had been broken. Rommel couldn't understand it, and tried to figure it out even as he ran through the woods. But his reasoning abilities were not the greatest anyway. Chuck was the thinker, the strategist. Chuck was, as much as Rommel hated to admit it, the brains of the team.

But as he approached the building, suddenly he felt it again. Something had happened; something had disrupted their communion. Perhaps even rendered Chuck unconscious. But now Chuck was—

Rommel froze. *RUN!* screamed his mind. *RUN! RUN! RUN!*

And that was when the building exploded.

Concussive force combined with waves of pure heat hurled Rommel back, back into the supposed safety of the woods. He tumbled tail over head, his fur crisping in the heat. He howled as he fell, and huge pieces of mortar and concrete plummeted all about him. It was nothing short of miraculous that he wasn't crushed by a piece of debris.

He kept on rolling, his paws scrabbling for purchase, finding none. The massive dog was completely in the power of something that utterly dwarfed him. He smashed into a tree, his head striking it with a sickening crunch, and that stopped him.

Consciousness fled him, and as it did, pieces of burning metal fell into the leaves overhead, embedded themselves in the trees.

All around the unmoving dog, trees began to burn.

6

Chuck felt a distant pain in his forehead, and was irritated with it . . . until he remembered that he should be dead, and therefore that pain was wonderful. It meant he was alive.

Except . . . what if he was, in fact, dead. And one could feel pain even in death. Now *that* hardly seemed fair. Then again, life had never been fair. Why should death be any different?

Slowly he raised his hand and felt what seemed to be caked blood on his forehead. He sat up carefully, uncertainly, his head throbbing. His fingers traced the line of the gash across him. Then he looked at the wall. There was a hole in it about the size of an acorn, and he was certain that there was a bullet inside that hole.

Shai had missed.

"The hell he did," said Chuck, staggering to his feet. He knew instinctively that Shai was a crack marksman. He had done precisely what he wanted to do, namely crease Chuck's skull.

Why? That was obvious. Despite the orders of the man who was apparently his boss, Shai had had no desire to kill Chuck.

"He wanted to fight me," Chuck told no one, shaking his head slowly. God, what insanity. Not only reveling in violence, but actually sparing someone's life so that a violent encounter could be anticipated. Still, Chuck couldn't knock it. If it hadn't been for that rather curious move on Shai's part, Chuck would not have survived the encounter.

He staggered out into the hallway, his head ringing. He placed a hand against a gleaming wall and winced at his reflection. Not pretty. Not in the least. But as least he was there.

He concentrated, reached out, trying to use his senses and discovering that they were indeed working. He was detecting a problem area up ahead. Might it be that Jupiter guy? The one who seemed to have the power to short out his own psychic abilities? *Anything was possible . . . anything except,* he thought bleakly, *the likelihood of his getting out of the place in one piece.*

He had wondered going in whether even Extremists would destroy a building if they knew there were still people inside. That if he just warned them that the guard had a daughter somewhere in the building, they might hold off. But Jupiter's brutal order of Chuck's death cast those hopes aside.

He was running, letting instinct take over. His mind was screaming a warning at him. He wasn't sure what he was sensing, only that there was great danger.

Part of him—*the intelligent part,* he thought bleakly—wanted to turn and run. Wanted to get the hell out of there. God, he was no hero. He was no intrinsically brave man who always did the heroic thing. No superhuman muscle-bender, the type he'd seen in the Holos, dodging bullets and performing invincible deeds as long as the camera was rolling. He was just a guy, driven by desperation and a need to make sure that no one was hurt. Still, it was times like these that he desperately wished there were a director somewhere yelling "Cut!"

He staggered, nausea overwhelming him, his head throbbing. He had not recovered from the creasing and he leaned against a wall, fighting his stomach and losing. He heaved the remains of his earlier meal onto the floor, choking and gagging. It took long seconds, and when he'd finished, he automatically started looking for something to clean it up before he realized that he had to have other priorities at the moment.

He started to run again, closing his eyes to try to ward off dizziness. *Not a concussion, please, please,* he prayed, wondering if God happened to be paying the least bit of attention to him this bleak night. As if in answer, the thunder cracked overhead.

Where are they? he thought desperately. If he ran into them now, with a mouth like sandpaper and the stability of quicksand, he wouldn't last a minute. But he had no choice. He had to find the girl; he had to get the hell out of here . . .

He had to turn right. Right here, through this door. Something was telling him that. Some inner sense, some . . .

And suddenly he realized that it wasn't an inner sense.

It was the beeping.

He had been so rattled, so confused and ill, that he had not realized that there had been a steady, insistent beeping noise. Faint when he had first come around, but getting louder as he had automatically started running toward it.

It was in the room, just off to the right. He ran into the room, all the time thinking desperately, *Please, please let it be something simple, something trivial, some automatic gimmick . . .*

He ran to the middle of the room, arms flailing in random, confused circles, and he spun there in the middle, looking around, trying to find the source.

Chuck spotted it. The source of the beeping, the source of where the noise had begun and where it would very shortly end, the alpha and omega. Birth and death.

Death. Oh, God, death. It was a bomb. It was a goddamn bomb, and it had been attached and wired to some huge bank of equipment. Equipment that was built right into the *wall*, and the bomb was ticking down. There it was, the LED reading and it said 008. Eight seconds.

"Eight . . . *seconds*!" Chuck screamed, as if arguing with the evidence of his own eyes.

They had been too thorough. This machinery it was wired to was humming with a low and powerful energy. It was a generator of some sort, that had to be it, and in a sense of perverse justice, it was powering the very bomb that was to be its instrument of destruction.

If he used his TK to rip out the bomb, that would set it off anyway. And in the time that it took for that information to sink in, three seconds had passed. Five seconds left.

No time, his mind screamed, and somewhere far in the distance he suddenly became aware of Rommel as his mind shouted, *Run! Run! RUN!*

He had already turned and dashed for the window, the power of his TK giving him an additional launch as if he'd hit a springboard and hurtled himself forward. The girl, wherever she was, was dead. There was nothing he could do. He sent a brief prayer heavenward for the girl's soul and, while he was at it, one for his own.

He smashed into the window and bounced off.

Bounced off.

He fell to the ground, glanced back reflexively. Two seconds.

His brain screamed and the scream blew out the window, shattering it into a million fragments. He leaped through the window, bringing his arms up to cushion the fall, and he glanced back, ignoring his mind that said, *Don't glance back, you idiot,* and the building blew.

White, incandescent light reached him first, searing his eyes, and he clapped his hands to his face and screeched, even as his shoulder hit the ground. He had had the briefest glance of woods far off to his left, the merest hint before the light cleansed his retinas.

A split instant later the heat hit him, but by then he was rolling, tumbling as was Rommel some distance away. But Rommel had been farther from the explosion. For Chuck the only salvation came in the rain. The rain, which had been his enemy, now allied itself, cooling him even as his skin puckered and blistered under the intensity.

Then came another explosion as, from somewhere within, another generator blew. The sky became a dazzling display, as if somehow lightning were no longer content to strike down from the clouds but were instead erupting up from the ground. If it had not been so horrifying it would have been glorious. If Chuck had been able to see he would have gasped in awe of the destructive toys mankind was capable of producing.

But he could see nothing. Instead he tumbled, helplessly, hopelessly, screaming and sobbing his pain and anguish and shock. A piece of cement caught him on the shoulder with the speed of a missile and he felt the shoulder go numb.

Waves of shock hurtled him farther, farther, the ground sloping precipitously. He tried to find the calm center of his soul, to allow the fates to carry him, but he was rattled, fighting for survival in the center of a hellish storm created by human hands.

He hit something, some sort of wooden railing, which crumbled so easily that he had a feeling it had been there for quite some time. A barrier, long ignored. But a barrier against what?

In less than a second he had his answer as the ground vanished from under him.

Just like that, there was no support. He was in midair, and even though his eyes were throbbing orbs rather than functioning instruments, he knew what had happened. He'd rolled off a cliff, a cliff that stood majestically above a river he'd seen out a bay window . . .

Back a few minutes ago. Back when he had sight. Back when he was alive. Not like now. Now was now, and now he had no sight, and now he was dead. He was a dead man.

He started to fall and he screamed. Not verbally, for his throat had constricted in panic, his vocal cords closing up. But his mind screamed, a primal bellow of pure terror that only comes when you are certain your life is over. Not endangered or grotesquely inconvenienced, but simply and irrevocably over.

His arms and legs spun, grasping at nothing, and he probably looked pretty damned funny, he realized.

And then gravity seized hold of him, and he fell.

7

DAKOTA WATCHED IN openmouthed astonishment as the explosion reached upward, the flames seeming to lick the heavens. First the light and then, moments later, the sound reached them, earsplitting and massive. Dakota staggered, unable to look away from it, her mouth moving but no words emerging.

"You bastards," she whispered before the noise had even begun to die down, and then more loudly, *"You bastards!"* She leaped toward Jupiter, fingernails bared, lips drawn back into a snarl. It was actually a fair impression of Rommel, and not intentional.

Also not particularly effective, for Jupiter did not back down in the least. Indeed he didn't have to, because a sharp and angry barking emerged from the van that brought Dakota up short.

A snapping, snarling Doberman came from the passenger's side, striking a defensive posture between the unflappable Jupiter and the hesitant Dakota. It took a step toward her and seemed ready to rip her to shreds. The only thing deterring it was Jupiter's firm but gentle hand on the back of its neck.

It brought Dakota's forward motion to a halt, but not her fury. "You blew up that place!" she said furiously. "Are you saying Chuck was in that place?"

"Of course," said Jupiter deferentially. "It was his own

fault he was in the wrong place at the wrong time . . . or
. . . was it just bad luck?''

"You lousy, lousy bastards!" Dakota was screaming, her
body trembling, her hands curled into shaking fists. But Jupiter was barely paying attention, instead studying her with a
casual detachment.

"Of course," he said in a triumphant whisper. "Oh, of
course. That explains everything."

Thunder rumbled as Jupiter advanced on her, and Dakota
started to back up, staggering. Then she shrieked as the dog
lunged forward, his jaws snapping on her pants leg.

"Get him off!" she howled.

"I don't suggest you go any farther," said Jupiter politely,
"or otherwise Mars will be forced to keep your calf as a
souvenir."

"Get him off get him off *get him off*!"

"You *are* the shrill one," said Jupiter, grabbing her firmly
by the wrist and gesturing Mars away. The Doberman backed
down, still growling, a piece of fabric from Dakota's pants
leg still in his teeth.

Jupiter yanked her forward, hard, and she cried out, stumbling on her injured ankle. Jupiter was supporting the weight
of her and when he spoke it was in an unhurried, but deadly
sounding, whisper. "I know who you are," he said softly,
"I know what you are. I know who you work for. And you
might prove valuable to us for a time before we're forced to
kill you. So come along."

He dragged her toward the back of the van, Dakota putting
up resistance as best she could. But it wasn't much as he
yanked open the doors. Darkness yawned at her and she
gasped as she made out two more forms within, and the brief
flash of the barrel of a gun.

"Welcome," said a deep voice with a faint Jamaican lilt.

Jupiter hurled her into the van and slammed the doors behind her, cutting off the sound of her shriek. He then came
quickly around the other side, and as he had expected, the

sounds of her protest had quickly been terminated, thanks to a gag that someone—probably Luta—had shoved in her mouth.

"Drive, Buzz," he said briskly.

Buzz fired up the engine, putting the van into gear, and he started down the roadway.

"Who the hell is she?" said Luta from the back, sounding extremely irritated. Luta did not take well to strangers at all.

"Remember our little discussion about the Complex?" asked Jupiter. "About how they nailed Porky?"

"Yeah. So?"

"I think this young woman is with the Complex."

In the darkness Dakota's eyes widened. She shook her head furiously, and her reward for it was a brisk crack against her skull by Luta.

"You think so?" Shai now rumbled.

"Fairly certain."

"How did you come up with that?"

"Well, we're fairly certain that the guy she's looking for is the guy whom I had Shai kill."

Shai remained stonily silent, and Jupiter did not give it any thought as he continued, "And that guy . . . he was something special. TK with remarkable power. I could barely hold him back. Plus hand-to-hand. And he was in exactly the right place at the wrong time, for us."

"But I still don't see—" Buzz began.

Jupiter quieted him with an impatient wave of his hand. "The rumor lately is about the psionics division the Complex has put together. That guy with the beard, he sure seemed like he would be right at home in an outfit like that. My guess is that somehow they caught wind of our plan and dispatched a team to try to check us out."

"She psionic too, then?" demanded Luta. She looked down a trifle nervously at Dakota, who was moaning softly because of the crack on the head she'd been given.

"I don't think so," said Jupiter slowly. "If she were, then I'd sense it. And—"

Suddenly he sat forward in alarm. "Buzz!"

The headlights of the van had picked up an unexpected sight. Ahead of them on the side of the road, was a squad of soldiers. One of the soldiers was in the forefront and was putting up a hand, indicating that the van should slow to a halt. From nearby now were visible the shining hand lamps of other soldiers as well.

Buzz slammed his hands down repeatedly on the steering wheel. "Goddamn!" he shouted over and over, and then turned and snarled at Jupiter. "You said they wouldn't get here this fast!"

"They shouldn't have," said Jupiter in obvious irritation. "They must have been in the area anyway."

"That's great! That's fuckin' great! We're screwed now, man! We're screwed!"

"Slow down," said Jupiter with icy calm. "Make them think we're cooperating."

Obediently, without comprehending, Buzz slowed the vehicle down. The speed dropped, the van wavering slightly on the slick roads. From the darkness of the van's back, there was the unmistakable sound of a rifle being readied.

"That won't be necessary," said Jupiter. "You've forgotten our little short circuit. Luta, my sweet . . ."

Without further prompting Luta made her way forward, her lack of height not even forcing her to bend over. She kneeled down next to Jupiter so that her eyeline was just above the dashboard.

"Ever do guns?" he asked. "Because now's the time."

Luta took a slow breath, clearing her mind. Buzz, at the wheel, risked a glance down at her. She gave him the creeps. When he used his power he didn't have to go through all this rigmarole. Letting out her breath, Luta placed the palms of her hands together, fingers upright and in front of her, pressing hard against each other.

"Ready," she said. "But there's a lot of guns."

"Just do your best. It'll be fine."

"Fine!" said Buzz incredulously. "If there's a bullet in my brain because she couldn't nail all the guns, that's not going to be fine."

"They'll never hit that small a target," Luta told him sweetly.

"Get ready," said Jupiter, "we're almost there."

The van slowed to a crawl, and the soldier stepped confidently in front of them. He started to say something about the explosion.

"Now," said Jupiter.

Luta reached out, her gaze sweeping the array of weapons in front of her. And one by one, each and every one of the gun mechanisms started to fall apart.

"Weapons failure!" shouted Private Dorsch, who happened to be checking his RBG's ammo level.

The squad had been carrying state-of-the-art, latest issue. The RBGs were the newest thing, the niftiest thing. Everything on the bastards was electronic, controlled by computer microchip. Thermal control to avoid overheating, ammo counter, computer-generated maintenance that was constant to avoid jamming.

So when Dorsch looked at the ammo counter and saw it go from full clip to empty, he knew there was a problem.

Sergeant Mary Jo Sanderson spun, checking her own weapon. She was standing to the right, near the passenger side. Dorsch was directly in front of the vehicle, having ordered it to slow down, since Sanderson had ordered that any vehicle entering or departing the area was to be treated suspiciously. To her horror and confusion, her own RBG was reading the same thing. And now the thermal emissions control was starting to go haywire. There was an audible crackling as microcircuits began to overload and spit out voltage.

"What the hell—?!" she shouted.

* * *

"Good going!" said Jupiter. "Buzz, get us out of here."

Buzz slammed down on the gas pedal and the van leaped forward.

Dorsch barely had time to look up when the van crashed into him. Sanderson screamed his name but he didn't hear it, didn't hear anything as he was hurled off to the side. His body bounced once, twice, and then skidded to a halt, lying there in the rain like a broken puppet.

The other soldiers reacted automatically, bringing their RBGs to bear on the speeding van and pulling the triggers. Most of them got no response at all, although several of them were greeted with crackling and spitting noises.

Jo didn't understand what was happening and, at the moment, was not taking the time to try to figure it out. Instead she tossed aside the RBG and yanked out the ancient service automatic that she kept holstered at her hip. Unlike the RBG there was no handy targeting lock-on, but she didn't care. She wasn't even thinking about what she was doing, only reacting in a cold fury to what had happened to Dorsch. She emptied the clip at the speeding van and, when it kept going, muttered a curse.

Others had already run over to Dorsch, who was lying there unmoving. Sanderson holstered the gun and ran over to the group of men who were rapidly checking Dorsch over. Winkowski looked up at her as she approached, and the expression on his face said it all.

"Let me through," she snarled. "Goddammit, Winkowski, out of the way." She pushed him aside and dropped down next to Dorsch, ready to apply CPR, first aid, mouth-to-mouth . . . anything that she could do so that she wouldn't have to admit that she had lost a man.

But one look at Dorsch told the entire story. His head was twisted at an impossible angle, his eyes still open in glazed surprise. Jo Sanderson bit her lower lip for a moment, but only a moment. Then steely resolve overtook her, and she reached over and closed Dorsch's unseeing eyes for him. "I'm sorry, Dorsch," she whispered. "Those bastards . . ." She turned and said to the men, "Did anyone get the plate number?"

"It didn't have one," said Winkowski and added indignantly, "That's illegal."

She looked at him with a touch of incredulity. "You're right. Gee, they might get in trouble."

Another soldier, Tang, pulled a blanket out of his duffel. Sanderson was puzzled until he reached over and spread it over Dorsch's body, obscuring it and protecting it from the rain. Sanderson gave a quick, approving nod.

Then from behind them someone—Murray—called out, "Sergeant! Check this out! I think you nailed 'em."

Jo rose quickly and went to where Murray was standing. On the ground in front of him were signs of skid marks that the van had left behind when it crashed into Dorsch. There was also a dark liquid, a series of splotches that ran down the road and into the distance.

"You hit something," said Murray. "Fuel line, maybe. Something. They're leaving a trail anyone can follow."

"They must be the ones who did the laboratory," said Jo briskly, trying to restore her mind to a businesslike mode in the wake of Dorsch's brutal slaying. "All right. Fall in. Now listen up," she said as they formed a semicircle around her, like a football team in a huddle. "If they're leaking fuel, they won't be able to get far. And I don't want to take chances that this rain is going to wash it away. I want the bastards who killed Dorsch." There were grim nods from all around, and she continued, "You three—Thompson, Koenig, Ingersoll—you head over to the plant. See if there's anyone still around, any survivors. Inspect the damage site, see what you can find. The rest of you, come with me."

"Shouldn't we check in with base?" asked Koenig.

"We're out of range," she said tightly, and indeed they probably were. They had been airlifted into the woods for survival and night training. They weren't scheduled to be picked up at their rendezvous point for two days.

Besides, part of Jo didn't want help even if they could get it. She was burning with cold fury over what had happened to Dorsch, and she knew that it had to be her and her squad who evened the scales for this crime. It had to be, or there was simply no justice in the world.

She glanced over in the direction of the explosion and saw to her dismay that the forest within the perimeter was burning. She had already pegged the work as that of Extremists. How ironic that people who proclaimed themselves concerned about the environment would commit an act that so flagrantly destroyed living trees.

In the forest that surrounded the site of the former lab, Rommel whined softly and lifted his head.

All around him the trees were going up in soaring towers of flame. The heavy rain was helping somewhat, preventing the fire from spreading and indeed diminishing its effects. If it weren't for the rain, Rommel, along with the entire forest, would have been consumed by this point.

Rommel staggered to his feet and reached out with his mind, trying to sense Chuck's whereabouts. He could detect nothing. Chuck was out of range, or unconscious. That Chuck might be dead, probably was dead, did not even occur to Rommel. Perhaps he might have somehow known instinctively if Chuck had met his demise. Or perhaps the thought of the man dying was simply inconceivable. The man was a constant, was a part of Rommel's life, and the dog didn't have the imagination to envision Chuck departing from it.

He started to make his way through the fire, stepping gingerly over burning branches. The trees burned angrily all around him, and the air was sizzling. His fur was soaked in some places, singed in others.

A crackling from overhead alerted him, and he leaped just in time to avoid a huge, fiery branch that plunged to the ground right where he had been only moments before. He glanced back, shaking his great head. Clearly this was not going to be easy.

He threaded carefully through, going as quickly as he could and fighting the urge to simply dash pell-mell through the forest. And finally he was out.

He stopped and stood there, panting rapidly, looking around for some sign of Chuck. But he knew there wouldn't be any. If Chuck were present he would sense it before he saw it. But he had to find Chuck, he simply had to.

Otherwise . . .

Who was going to feed him?

8

CHUCK PLUNGED DOWN, down toward the river far below.

Once before he had tried to use his power to break a fall, and had not been particularly successful. But that time he had been able to see, and had partially been frozen by the sheer magnitude of looking down and seeing the drop that awaited him.

This time his main handicap was also his only advantage. He had no ability to look down, devastated as his vision was by the explosion. So instead, in his desperation, his TK power lashed out wildly, even as he free-fell. He sought out the ground, not able to see it, but trying to *feel* it, feel the hardness of it so that he could push against it.

He kept falling, plummeting, trying to slow himself down. He clutched at his throat, feeling hopeless panic trying to lock into his mind and paralyze it, gravity pulling him down hungrily, eager to assert its dominance.

And his fingers grasped on something around his neck, something he'd gotten so used to that he had forgotten he was wearing it. The spoon that he wore around his neck that had been bent, through the power of his mind, into an oddly shaped letter *A*. The first letter of his ex-wife's first name.

He whispered it, like a prayer, trying to pull strength from it, trying to center on it and fight the confusion and disorientation. Was he ten feet above the ground? A hundred? A thousand? And suddenly he realized he was slowing. Not much, not much at all . . . maybe barely enough to fight the acceleration that was part of a falling body. But something.

Would it be enough? If he hit ground, going at the speed he was, would he survive? Probably not. Probably not. He was dead. That was all. Even as he refocused his will, fought to slow himself down further, despair was surging through him. And yet, the more he despaired, the more perversely determined he became.

In the distance he heard a sound, like roaring from a great wind tunnel. No . . . not wind. Water . . .

And then he plunged into the river.

He gasped as he hit, giving him barely a lungful of air before he sank beneath the surface. He flailed about desperately, becoming disoriented and unsure of which way was up or down. He went down, down, and then struck the bottom of the riverbed, thereby determining for certain which way was which.

His feet sank into the muck and he pulled them free, then kicked upward. The fierce current of the river was already pulling him, and the brief amount of air in his lungs was already running out. He felt a sharp pain in his chest as it demanded air, trying to force him to breathe, oblivious and uncaring of the fact that he was underwater.

He swam as hard as he could, no slick, organized paddling but instead a desperate attempt to reach the surface. He flailed desperately, the river buffeting him about . . .

And then, to his astonishment, he broke the surface.

His lungs sucked in air greedily and then he went under again, but this time there was no panic, not even the need to fight off panic. Now there was simply quiet and determined desperation as he swam with fierce, sure strokes. He had been a gym coach, for pity's sake. One of the best athletes in his town. He could handle this, blast it.

But the disorientation of the blackness that surrounded him was a powerful thing, a frightening thing. He tried to ignore it, but how can one ignore the inescapable? Even as he swam as hard as he could, he realized with dull horror that he had no idea what direction he was going. The water was sweeping him along as uncaringly as if he were a branch or twig. All around him was darkness, and the roaring of the river that was everywhere. As the river had tried to fill his lungs, unsuccessfully, the pure noise and power of it did indeed succeed in filling what remained of his senses.

But he refused to give up, refused to surrender, and he swam desperately and furiously. He didn't know where he was going but dammit he was going to get there in a hurry.

He lost track of time. He might have been swimming forever. He might have always been swimming. Perhaps everything he had ever thought he had done was simply an illusion, and he had actually been spending his entire existence anxiously paddling in some godforsaken river in Colorado.

The roaring ahead of him grew louder and he didn't understand why, so caught up was he in a flow of crazed thoughts. Of course, it was understandable why the increase in sound held no particular meaning for him.

He had never seen a waterfall.

But he certainly felt it as once again the world dropped out from under him and he plummeted. Fortunately—if that term could reasonably be used to describe any part of his current state of affairs—it was a short waterfall. Moments after he'd gone over the edge he hit the bottom of it. He went under for a moment, the strength of the waterfall pressing him down, but then he bobbed to the surface, splashing about and gasping for air once more.

His desperate fingers found something, a branch, and his hand closed around it. And to his amazement, the branch didn't move. Instead it anchored him to the spot, despite the river's best efforts to continue to sweep him away.

He continued just holding on for a few moments, making sure for himself that the branch was really not going to go anywhere. Then he began to pull himself toward shore, hand over hand. He tried to ignore the blackness, the coldness in his body, the rasping of his breath, and the steady, infernal noise of the river. He tried to ignore it all, focusing entirely on the branch. His salvation, his only friend in the world, was this piece of wood.

A piece of bark came away in his hand, but he managed to reaffirm his grip and hold on, just hold on. Then his feet touched the riverbed, gave him purchase and support, and he pushed along, pulling himself hand over hand even faster now. Hope gave him additional strength, and within moments, he was on the shore.

He lay there for a long time, gasping for air, his heart pounding. He was drenched, his clothes sopping, his hair plastered down. Although he couldn't see it, some of the dye he used in his hair to cover the blondness had washed away, leaving his head somewhat mottled-looking, But he wouldn't have cared, just as he didn't care about the coldness and dampness. All he cared about was that he was on the land and he was safe.

Safe.

Slowly he sat up and started to assess precisely what was meant by "safe."

He was blind. The cold harshness of that began to set in as he passed his hand in front of his face and saw nothing, not even the slightest motion of shadows. Even when he was a kid, playing inane party games that required a blindfold, he was still able to see something. Some vague hint, some distinguishing between light and dark. Of course, it was nighttime, which didn't help. Still . . .

And he was alone in the forest. A forest that was, if Jupiter could be believed, filled with creatures that had been mutated by chemicals dumped into . . .

The river. And now he shivered reflexively. If it was true—if there were chemicals in the river—had they had an effect on him? Maybe. Maybe. Maybe it took a long time to affect you. The animals drank there all the time, after all. Maybe his immersion in it would be harmless, have no ill effects at all. Maybe . . .

Maybe . . . and maybe he was going to die. Maybe he was going to change, or display the effects of radiation poisoning. Maybe his hair would fall out or his tongue turn into some mottled green thing. Maybe . . .

Maybe he was going to make himself crazy if he kept this up.

He stood slowly, on unsteady legs. He staggered, never realizing how much he depended on sight to do something as simple as walk. Suddenly the entire world had become something he approached tentatively, if at all. Part of his instinct told him to just sit and wait for someone to come for him . . .

Dakota. The poor woman, she was sitting back in the truck, waiting for him to come with help. He couldn't even help himself, and now there was someone else depending on him.

And Rommel . . .

And somehow, instinctively, Chuck knew that Rommel was no longer in the truck. He didn't know how he knew, and for that matter, he didn't know where Rommel was. But he wasn't in the truck. He hadn't sat around waiting for Chuck to return. He was . . . where?

Where, for that matter, was Chuck?

He began to walk, every step cautious and uncertain. He was positive that he was going to step on a branch or a rock and fall over, or be attacked by some sort of wild beast. He felt eyes, millions of eyes, staring at him from the woods, and he was certain they weren't really there, but couldn't shake the feeling that they were. And as it whirled around in his mind, he tripped over a branch.

He lay there for a moment, then sat up, brushing the dirt off his hands. Then he reached out, his hands moving in formless patterns until his fingers closed around the branch that had just tripped him up. It was long, four and a half feet at least, maybe five.

He stood, picking up the branch. Then he held it out just in front of him, tip near the ground, and started to walk. He moved the branch in front of him as if it were a radar sweeper, and it worked perfectly, detecting high branches or small holes that could trip him up.

He walked down the shore, looking for help, trying to ignore the bone-chilling coldness that cut to his marrow.

9

"WE GET OUR stuff and we get the hell out," said Buzz, stalking the interior of their cramped hideout.

"I agree," said Shai from the darkness, which was unusual for Shai. More often than not he would reject a suggestion from Buzz out of hand, simply because of the source. But there was something about Shai now, something that had Jupiter a bit concerned.

Jupiter sat cross-legged on the floor, stroking his chin thoughtfully. "Luta?" he said. "Your thoughts on the matter?"

"Whatever you say is fine, Jupiter."

"That wasn't my question," he gently remonstrated her.

There was a pause and a sigh from the darkness. "What do we do about her?"

It was the way Luta had of answering questions. When she was certain that the course of action was already decided, she would respond with a question about the next step to be taken.

The "her" referred to, of course, was tied up in the corner. Dakota felt the dull, throbbing ache in her ankle now, which matched the pain in her head from when that small woman had knocked her cold. Her lips thinned in annoyance. She'd love to be able to go a couple of rounds with that little sleaze without some sort of handicap. "Yes," she said in annoyance. "What about me?"

Jupiter did not respond at first, instead staring off into space, his fingers steepled in front of him. "You, my dear . . . you will be coming with us."

There were murmurs of surprise and irritation from the others in the group. Buzz, naturally, was the loudest, as he snapped, "What in hell we need her for?"

"For protection."

"Protection? Us? What the hell do we need protecting from?"

Luta, naturally, promptly took Jupiter's side and said to Buzz sarcastically, "You didn't sound so confident when you were staring down the soldiers' rifles."

"Yeah, well . . . you did fine with that," he admitted grudgingly. "But that just proves my point. Why don't we just ditch her or kill her or something. Why drag her along?"

"We only kill when we have to," said Shai.

There was a polite cough from Jupiter in response to that. "Oh, is that a fact?"

"Yeah."

"Shai," he said as if addressing a child, "you're obviously forgetting something. The government will not operate under such strictures. If they find us, they'll kill us. Make no mistake about that. Even if we're unarmed. Even if we surrender. That is how things are done nowadays, and that's how we must respond."

"Nice excuse," said Dakota. Her initial fear had been replaced by a burning anger, by a frustration that control over her life had been usurped in this way.

Jupiter slowly turned his gaze on her. "Considering, my dear, that you are the one benefiting from this course of action, I find your arrogance ill-timed and misplaced. As just another corpse you are eminently disposable. It is only your connection with the Complex, and your possible use as a bargaining chip, that enables you to continue breathing."

"Oh, really. And what if I—"

She stopped. She could continue to protest that she wasn't

part of the Complex, but she realized that one of two things would happen. Either they wouldn't believe her, or they would. If they didn't believe her, then she was wasting her breath. If they did believe her . . . they would waste her. So it dawned on her that completing the sentence might not be the smartest thing to do in regards to her continued health.

So she quickly changed tactics and said, "And what if I scream?"

"Go right ahead," said Jupiter. "But we're somewhat isolated in this cabin. That's why we chose it. No one will hear you."

She sat there, steaming. When it became obvious to Jupiter that she was not going to say anything further, he nodded curtly and said, "All right, Buzz. Go load up the van."

"Why do I have to do all the shit work?" he demanded. From nearby Mars growled, sharing Buzz's irritation.

"Because you're the biggest shit," said Luta sweetly.

He grunted as he got up. When he had walked out the door, Jupiter said to Dakota, "What do you think of our little group?"

"I think you're monsters," she replied sharply.

"Indeed. And tell me, my dear . . . have you wondered why winters are so mild these days? Hmmm? Have you wondered why 'Dangerous Breathing' days have become more and more frequent? Why skin cancer is on the rise, not to mention a number of other bizarre medical situations that people can't readily explain?"

"No."

"Of course not." He smiled, but the smile did not touch his eyes. "You're not meant to wonder. You're a good little drone. The government doesn't want you to wonder, and so you don't. The government wants you to sign over your independence and your loyalty and your mind, and you do so willingly. Take your best shot, my dear, at calling me names. I can assure you that the names I can call you are far more disturbing."

"More disturbing than 'murderer,' " she said tightly.

"Life ends, my dear . . . what is your name, anyway?"

"Screw you."

"Very well. Life ends, my dear Screw. Sooner or later, all life ends. But what you do with your mind, and with your time here on earth—that is the most important thing. And it's my overall accomplishments that should—"

He was stopped by an angry shout from outside, and the sounds of pounding footsteps as Buzz ran back into the house, a string of profanities leaping from his lips.

"What's happened?" demanded Jupiter, trying to cut it short.

"We have no fuel!" shouted Buzz, waving his hands about.

"Impossible."

"Not impossible! Those bastards winged the van somehow. There's a neat little hole in the tank, and every drop leaked out; most on the way up here, the rest in a nice puddle while we were parked. Now how the hell are we gonna get out of here?"

"We'll have to find and steal another vehicle, that's all—" Jupiter's voice trailed off as clearly something upsetting occurred to him. Dakota could imagine what it was, for the same thing was crossing her mind as well.

"Damn," said Shai, also realizing.

"What? What is it?" said Buzz, looking from one to the other.

"If we've been leaking fluid all the way back here . . ." said Jupiter.

"Then we left them a trail, Jupe," finished Shai. "And the rain's tapered off . . . probably didn't even begin to wash the stuff away."

"They'll come after us," said Jupiter. "They'll know we couldn't have gotten far. Even on foot, they'll be here before too long."

"We have to stop them!" said Luta in alarm. "Jupiter, do something!"

Jupiter was stroking his chin thoughtfully. "I won't have to," he said after a time. "Buzz will."

"We're dead," said Shai.

Buzz looked at him with indignation. "What, you think I can't?"

"I think we're dead is all I'm saying."

"Well, the hell with you," snapped Buzz. "You think I can't? I'll show you who can't."

Jupiter smiled to himself. It was a ritual that they commonly engaged in. Buzz seemed to lack the concentration to simply go ahead and use his ability. He always seemed to need someone like Shai to push him and prod him, to tell him that he was incapable, so that he could rise to the occasion. Jupiter suspected that it was probably something sexual. Then again, so was most of life.

Buzz sat down on the floor and started to concentrate. He made sure not to engage in any of the deep-breathing nonsense that Luta seemed constrained to do. Instead, he simply concentrated, reaching out to the immediate area to see what he could find.

He touched the most sensitive mind first and blinked in surprise. A voice seemed to sound in his head, and it said, *Chuck, is that you?* and he had no idea what it meant. But he didn't like the sound of it, not at all, and so he quickly withdrew his mind and moved on. And then he started to locate the types he was looking for. Minds of simplicity, of free-floating anger and pure instinct. Minds that he could control and guide.

He told them what he wanted them to do, who to look for. He told them what it would take to please him. And in that silent communion they agreed, eager to obey and earn his approval. For Buzz had instilled in their makeup, with but the slightest effort, that getting his approval was immensely important.

* * *

Rommel had squeezed his massive frame back through the fence and had begun a steady, distance-consuming lope that brought him back in short order to the pickup truck they'd left behind. It sat there on the side of the road, abandoned and lonely. Rommel was confused. Bad enough that Chuck had disappeared. Now where had the woman gone? In terms of communication she was less than useless, but she might be able to feed him at least. But she was nowhere to be found. Typical human. Always underfoot when you don't need them, never around when you do.

Suddenly Rommel looked up, as if a voice had called down to him from on high. He glanced around in confusion and whined softly. He had heard a voice in his mind. It didn't sound like Chuck, didn't feel like him . . . but Chuck's was the only voice that had ever entered his head before.

Chuck, is that you? he asked.

And then, just like that, it was gone. Rommel couldn't understand it. Automatically he put his nose to the ground and made a circle of the pickup truck, trying to detect a scent. As if he were certain that there had been a human being standing there and was now, for some strange human reason, hiding. Not that it made any sense, but then humans never seemed to be overly concerned about making sense.

But there was nothing. Not a damned thing.

He barked loudly, and then howled, in hopes that a response would come. But none did.

He stayed by the truck a while longer, and then started down the roadway. He kept up a brisk, steady trot . . . and then picked up something. A scent, faint, but there. The scent of humans, a lot of them. It was possible, with so many spoors mixed together, that Chuck's was among them. Humans had a habit of hanging out with each other. Rommel wasn't entirely sure why. He could barely handle being around two at the most. So what in the world someone would want with a lot of them was beyond him.

Nevertheless, Chuck might be with them. And so he set out at a steady run, picking up speed as the spoor grew stronger. His stomach rumbled in irritation. He hoped he would find some food soon, because he was starting to feel as if he'd be willing to eat the first thing he saw.

As it happened, the first thing he saw was a body.

He stopped in surprise. Not just a body. A couple of bodies. He swung his massive head around, his large eyes taking it all in.

They looked vaguely familiar. Then he remembered. They were dressed similarly to the humans in that place that Chuck had called—what was it—the Complex. Where Chuck and he had met. They were the men with the rifles who tried to stop Rommel and Chuck from leaving. Soldiers. Rommel had gotten to ride a motorcycle that time. It had been fun and Chuck had promised him that he might get to do it again someday. So far, he hadn't.

These men were different soldiers, and they had no motorcycles. They didn't even have lives. Something, something with an unnatural scent, had ripped them apart. Rommel did not like the look of it at all, because as near as he could tell, whatever had killed the men would probably not have much trouble killing a certain German shepherd either.

Still . . . at least there was food here.

His jaws hovered over the body of one of the humans, ready to rip off some meat . . .

And he hesitated.

Now what in the world was holding him back? Chuck wasn't around to be that damnable voice that restrained him. Theoretically nothing should be preventing him from chowing down. It's not like the human needed the meat anymore, after all.

So why was it that he could picture Chuck in his mind, an angry finger waving at him, saying, "No, Rommel. Not that. You can't eat that. I won't like it, and I wouldn't want you to."

Why did he give a stale dog biscuit what Chuck would say?

Chuck got in his way half the time. Chuck was this irritating lock on him, a human choke collar. Chuck was . . .

Chuck would be . . .

Chuck would be disappointed in him.

He growled low in his throat. Hell, it wasn't like the human was going to attack him, or even would attack him anytime in the future. This was a seriously dead human, and so were his friends. So it could not remotely be considered self-defense, or disabling or killing an attacker. It was just meat.

Just meat.

And he couldn't do it. He was hungry and tired and furious with himself, but he couldn't do it.

In annoyance, he urinated around the corpses. Just in case he changed his mind. But he had the dismal feeling he wasn't going to.

That's what happens when you hang around with humans, he realized. It spoils you.

There was the further scent of humans past that point, though, mingled with the scent of the other creature. Rommel followed the scent, which led him deep into bushes and trees. Except that they had been knocked down, torn about. Something had come through here with the speed and power of a bulldozer, and Rommel had the distinct feeling he knew what it was. It was the same creature that had killed the humans behind him.

He followed the scent all the way, as far as he could, before he stopped.

The scent of the humans—no, one human, he now realized—ended here. And ''here'' was a cliff, jutting out over a sheer drop. The wind whistled fiercely around it, buffeting Rommel so hard that he did not dare to go to the edge of the cliff and look over. It wasn't really necessary. He knew exactly what he would find—a drop so steep that no human could possibly survive it.

There were tracks as well, tracks that led to the edge of the cliff and away. There was no doubt in Rommel's mind that they were tracks from whatever the creature was that had killed the hu—

His ears suddenly pricked up. Something was approaching from behind him, downwind of him so that he hadn't caught the scent sooner. And then came a roar so deafening that Rommel almost leaped right off the edge of the cliff in response. As it was the explosive noise startled him so greatly that he leaped from hiding and skidded halfway toward the cliff edge.

He spun and stared incredulously at what was coming at him.

It was a bear, but far more massive than any he had ever seen. And it looked—wrong. Its fur was wrong, its eyes, its whole manner. It smelled wrong. It was dying. That was it. It was dying, except the bear didn't know it yet. And it was a slow death. Might take weeks or months before the bear would notice that it was dying, at which point it would probably just keel over.

Unfortunately it was nowhere near that time yet.

The slavering monster lunged toward Rommel. Rommel waited until it was almost upon him, then dodged around him like lightning. The bear staggered and then turned. By that point, however, Rommel had darted back into the woods. He had seen everything he wanted to see, everything that he was going to see.

Rommel briefly considered the idea of fighting the bear, but that seemed an exercise in futility, if not outright suicide. So instead he elected to run, assuming that, if he couldn't outfight the damned thing, at the very least he could outrun it.

But as he ran through the woods, he wondered what in the world had caused the bear to look like that. And he also wondered if somehow the human whom the bear had stalked to the cliff had somehow managed to survive. Humans, Rommel realized, could be very resourceful when they weren't being self-absorbed.

10

AT THE POINT in time when Rommel had first returned to the pickup, and was briefly waiting for either Dakota or Chuck or both to return, Sergeant Mary Jo Sanderson was leading her squad in pursuit of the individuals she believed to have been responsible for the bombing of Internet Propulsion.

The dripping fuel had indeed been an invaluable means of tracking. The squad of a dozen men had broken camp earlier, and were carrying everything they'd brought with them when they'd first been airdropped down. Nevertheless, Jo noted with pride, it hadn't slowed them one iota.

She tried to figure out what in the world was going on. Why had there been massive weapons failure all at the same time? The odds of that happening were . . . well, there were no odds for it. It could not, should not happen, under any circumstances. But it had, robbing them of their standard heavy firepower. They still had their handguns, and some of those could be pretty high tech—especially the ones with the laser sighters. Jo, for her part, still preferred the old style one that she kept holstered. The one her father had used and had given her. She'd worn and fired it with pride, although her mother had shuddered every time she'd seen it being used.

"Sergeant!" came a voice from up ahead. It was Winkowski, she realized. He was the best tracker in the outfit, the one with the best eyesight. And it was clearly serving him in good stead now, for he said, "Over there. It goes off over there."

Sure enough, the droplets had veered off. It was a narrow dirt road, mostly obscured by bushes and overgrowth, and left to their own devices, Sanderson's squad might well have walked right past it.

Sanderson pulled out her gun and replaced the magazine, not satisfied with the fact that it was half empty. She slammed a new magazine in place, tucking the partially depleted one into her pocket. "Okay, people," she said, "you look alive and you stay alive. Shapp, you're on point."

The men nodded silently, making their own ammo checks. Then they entered the passage cautiously, two-by-two formation, with Shapp several feet ahead leading the way.

Shapp was one of the more experienced members of the squad, which was why it was a shame when he died first.

They had penetrated halfway up the overgrown road when a massive roar shook them to their roots. The squad froze, casting nervous glances at each other.

"What the hell was that, a fucking lion?" demanded Winkowski.

"Shapp, what do you see?" called Sanderson.

What Shapp saw was movement, to his right, something huge. He swung his pistol around and squeezed off four rounds, each explosion of his weapon deafening. And now the others following suit, pumping away at the same general direction that Shapp had been firing in. Like deadly fireflies, shots ripped through the air, lighting up the underbrush.

"Cease fire!" Jo called out. "Come on, hold it! Save ammo, goddammit!"

They obeyed her order and they paused, waiting to hear some movement, some sign of anything.

"Nothing could have survived that barrage," said Jo confidently.

Shapp never got a chance to agree or disagree, because a huge paw swept out from the underbrush. The first arc of the claw took off his face, and even as he keeled over dead, the return arc ripped out his bowels, sending blood and gore spilling to the dirt.

It leaped into their path. It was massive beyond massive, a grizzly from hell. On its body were the marks of the bullet wounds. It was bleeding from a dozen hits, and it didn't seem to be the least bit bothered by them.

It charged at them, bellowing defiance. They didn't hear Jo's screams of *"Fall back"* . . . they didn't need to hear them, because they were falling back just fine without any urging.

There was a snarl from behind them and Jo, who was bringing up the rear, spun. Her eyes widened in shock.

It was, of all things, a raccoon. A cute, furry raccoon, except it was about twice as large as any she had ever seen, and there was madness in its eyes. It leaped straight at them with incredible agility. Jo swung an arm, catching the creature's tail and hurling it to one side.

The raccoon snagged onto a branch and the branch bent and then snapped the creature right back at the soldiers. It sailed through the air and landed on the back of Private Dawson. Dawson screamed as the raccoon sank its teeth into the back of Dawson's neck and, with an effortless yank, ripped out Dawson's throat. Blood flew, spattering Jo and others around her.

In front of them the bear was tearing them to ribbons. Three men were already down, and the squad was emptying all its ammo into the bear. It wasn't even being slowed down. It grabbed a fourth man, lifted him high over its head, and Jo watched helplessly, in terror, as her man was ripped in half, in goddamn *half.*

From somewhere she heard Winkowski scream, *"Let's get the fuck out of here!"*

The squad broke and ran. They tried to retreat but now there were more creatures coming at them, squealing and

gibbering in high-pitched, insane caricatures of their own
voices. The soldiers split, ran any which way they could.

Jo was not ecstatic with the way her men were responding
to pressure. Then again, she couldn't blame them for two
reasons—first, this was beyond anything they'd ever been
trained to deal with. And second, she was busy running herself.

Mary Jo Sanderson plunged through the woods, smashing
through the branches that ripped at her face and clothes, running as fast as she could. She shouted the names of her men,
hoping to pull them together. But she got no response. Instead she heard screams, shouts of horror and fear, ripping
and chewing noises. She bit back tears, because dammit she
was too hard-bitten to cry, she had been through too much
to revert to some damned stereotype weepy female.

She saw a clearing up ahead and dashed for it. She broke
into an open area, kept on going, and skidded to a stop.

A cliff. A sheer drop. (The same cliff, in fact, that Rommel
would arrive at some time later.) She looked around, considered trying to climb down it, and promptly dismissed that
option as counterproductive to her continued existence.

A fierce wind was blowing around her, so fierce she staggered and almost lost her footing. It was as if some massive
hand wanted to pick her up and fling her to her doom.

The full horror and shock of what had happened had not
yet set in. For that she was grateful. In the distance she heard
shouts and screams. Her men. She had deserted her men. No
she hadn't, she had just run with the rest of them. But dammit, she was the leader. She should have done something.

She still could. Perhaps she still could.

She turned toward the woods and froze.

The bear was standing there, its mouth covered with gore.
She thought she saw a piece of someone's uniform sticking
in its teeth.

They stood there, studying each other for a moment, and
then the bear opened its mouth and roared.

She brought her gun up and emptied the remains of the magazine at the animal. It staggered slightly under the assault, but otherwise seemed uninjured, even angered. Nothing was stopping the huge beast, nothing.

Jo backed up until she could back no further. The wind yanked at her, and it was all she could do not to be blown away. But maybe that would be preferable, because the monster was advancing on her, waving its paws, ready to gut her as it had her men.

If only they had packed heavier firepower—but who could have predicted what had happened? Who knew their RBGs would go out? Who knew, when they'd been airdropped down for a routine survival—

Airdropped.

"My God," she whispered even as her hand flew to her pack. When they'd broken camp, she'd been a good soldier and packed up everything. Brought everything. Including her reserve parachute pack. She'd cut loose the parachute since it had gotten tangled in trees when they first landed. The parachute was gone. But not the new, light emergency chute, still clipped to her pack harness.

If she just jumped and opened it, it probably wouldn't slow her down in time to avoid getting killed. She wasn't high enough. But—

The bear roared and charged as she yanked on the emergency rip cord. The chute rippled out from her pack, and the high winds on the cliff grabbed it up and yanked her off. The bear skidded to a halt and stood there, confused and puzzled, as Jo was picked up by the winds and carted away.

She was carried high, high into the air, out of control, as she watched the cliff recede, the bear standing there in frustration. Then suddenly a downdraft caught her, sending her spiraling downward. She dangled helplessly, knocked about at the whim of the wind. She watched the ground pass under her with dizzying speed, and gasped as the breath was knocked out of her.

In front of her loomed trees, and she was heading straight for them. There was absolutely no way she could avoid them, for she was at the mercy of the wind, and the wind was not feeling especially merciful.

She crashed into the branches and they ripped at her, ripped at her parachute, tearing gaping holes in it. Jo Sanderson fell, branches cushioning her but breaking under her weight. She screamed in pain and frustration . . .

And hit the ground.

She lay there for a long moment, not daring to breathe, afraid that taking a breath would inform her that she had broken a rib or punctured a lung. But eventually she did indeed take a long, slow, deep breath.

Nothing. No sign of damage in the chest area. All right, she told herself, let's check the rest.

She stood slowly, carefully, on wobbly legs. She took stock of herself, checking all over for broken bones, but she couldn't find any. She was banged up and bruised, but otherwise seemed in fairly good shape.

There was the old saying, she recalled, that any landing you can walk away from is a good one. Well, this might not have been pretty. Indeed, it was pretty god-awful and undignified, but at least she was alive. And she was walking away from it, and by God, it was a good landing after all.

She took two steps and a roar filled the air.

She spun.

Another huge, mutant bear crashed out of the woods, heading right for her.

The last thing she had time to think before the animal got to her was, *So much for the good landing . . .*

11

SOMEHOW CHUCK'S SWEEPING, makeshift cane managed to miss a rather nasty tree root. Chuck's foot, however, did not, as he tripped over it and fell, sprawling, to the floor. As he fell, he accidentally dropped his cane and it rolled away from him, to sit serenely under a nearby bush.

It was only a little more than an arm's length away, but for Chuck it might as well have been a mile. He started to crawl around, reaching, trying to grasp it, and when several minutes of this yielded nothing, he stopped. He began to imagine what he had looked like just now, on hands and knees, trying to find a stick.

My God, he thought, *what if I have to spend the rest of my life like this?*

He had been trying to seal away the enormity of his predicament. To ignore it, to deal with it, just deal with it, rather than succumb to the massive difficulty of it. But that was no longer possible, and he fell to the ground and started to sob, his back heaving, tears rolling down his face. He was completely and utterly alone. No humans to help him, no dog to support him, lost and alone, completely alone. Just how dismal his fate was, he couldn't even begin to comprehend.

The realization that he just might not ever get out of these woods . . . that, indeed, it was likely he would not . . . was overwhelming. He'd heard of people who wandered in circles for days at a time, and they were sighted. And he was—

"Blind," he muttered harshly. The sound of his voice was the first human sound he'd heard in what seemed ages. He had completely lost track of time, but the world was terrifying to him. Simply terrifying. He never had any idea whether every single moment might be his last. Something might be watching him, getting ready at any time to leap out at him before he could stop it. He'd die there—

(Calm down.)

—his body gutted by whatever it was that killed him—

(Knock it off.)

—and left there, food for whatever other things happened to pass by and want a quick snack, as if he were a late-night deli—

(Christ almighty, stop it!)

—and his body would decompose, never found by a human being, and things would crawl in and out of it and—

(STOP IT!)

He screamed, an agonized, choking, sobbing scream that carried high into the trees, into the uncaring sky. The rain had trailed off, leaving him damp but getting no damper, and miserable, and alone—

He buried his face in his hands and continued sobbing. And when he had finished with that, had gotten it all out of his system, he let out a slow, trembling sigh. A cleansing breath to relax him and clear his mind.

Okay. He'd made a fool of himself. At least there was no one around. The only witness to his little display of histrionics were the trees, and the chances were slim that they were going to tell anyone.

Deal with it, Simon. Just deal with it.

He felt queasy and sick, probably from the water that he'd had to take a little ride through. He closed his eyes and searched for balance. Balance within himself. Balance with nature.

It was why he had taken up aikido in the first place. The low-level babble of the world that his untrained mind had picked up, like a radio with a broken receiver, had come close to driving him insane. He had become both a Quaker and a student of aikido to retrain his mind into the way of peace, into the way of calm and communion with nature, something that both philosophies emphasized.

Just because he was unable to see nature did not mean that it had departed from him. He was still himself. He had not lost the ability to remain in touch with himself, and that was what was important.

To reinforce the feeling of inner calm, Chuck stepped into his natural, relaxed stance, performed another cleansing breath. Then he began to do his *kata*, a pattern of movements that enabled him to run through the techniques of aikido. At first he felt the tentativeness and uncertainty of the moves, but he brought his concentration around to it, managed to focus. By the time he was running through the *kata* for the third time, he was performing with the speed and style to which he had grown accustomed.

He let out a sigh and kneeled, feeling some small measure of triumph at the reclamation of his spiritual center.

And from there, he was struck by an idea. One that he chided himself over not having realized earlier. If he walked in his usual manner, refusing to adapt to the situation that fate had dealt him, he was going to continue to fall. The farther he had to fall from, the more it was going to hurt.

But there was no real reason he had to walk the way he usually did.

Many techniques in aikido had been developed to defend oneself from attack while on one's knees—in the event that you were kneeling to someone who was secretly your enemy and they took that opportunity to try to kill you. But part of the techniques in defense was the *shikko*, the kneeling walk. It had never been contemplated as a means of getting around—merely something to be used in tandem with the kneeling techniques of the *suwari-waza*. But one did have to adapt to changing times.

From his kneeling position, Chuck raised his upper body and brought his left foot forward, knee up. Simultaneously he moved his right foot behind his left foot. Then he brought his left knee to the ground, advanced his right foot, also knee up, and this time brought his left foot behind his right foot. In this way, crablike, he moved across the ground.

To his right was the rushing river, and he decided to try to stick to that so that he needn't worry about going in circles. Not only that, but he wouldn't have to be concerned about being attacked from that side.

As he moved, he tried to sense with his mind rather than with his eyes. All around him, really, was peace and serenity. Rather than be afraid of it, he should try to embrace it.

Out of habit he was keeping his hands on his upper thighs, and so he banged his knee rather sharply against a tree that was directly in his path. He stopped, rubbing the knee to try to restore circulation, and as he did so, he tried to feel the tree. Not with his hands, but with his mind. He tried to reach out and feel the sense of it, the being of it. Get some sort of knowledge that it was there.

He couldn't. He wasn't sure what he was supposed to do. But he should be able to, should have some sense of the world beyond his eyes. After all, he picked things up with the power of his mind, envisioned their levitation and made it so. This wasn't much different, was it?

He reached out with his hands, feeling the surface of the tree, putting his hands around it, running his fingers over it. He nodded slowly, putting together in his mind an image of what he was facing. Then he leaned back, released his grip, and tried to see it without seeing it. Tried to imagine and remember what it had felt like, put the fragments together in his head.

He tried to see it without seeing it.

He couldn't. He knew in his heart that he hadn't gotten it yet. So he tried with something smaller, picking up a rock and palming it carefully, feeling the weight and heft of it. It was a particularly smooth one and his fingers caressed it. Then slowly he put the rock down and simply sat there, trying to call it to mind. He envisioned the rock, simple, small, and hard.

Then he did what he used to do when he was first learning how to use his power—he envisioned a giant hand doing his bidding. In his mind's eye, which was still sharp and clear, a large hand was stretching out, raising up the rock and bringing it over to just in front of his face.

Slowly, tentatively, he reached out to grasp the rock that was hovering there. His hand passed through the air, and there was nothing to impede it. He frowned, passed his hand in the other direction. Nothing.

He reached down and picked the rock up with his hand. It hadn't budged from where he'd left it.

This was not going to be easy. Not easy at all.

12

DAKOTA HAD BEEN silent witness to the screams and shouts from outside the cabin, the gunfire accompanied by the roaring and the hideous sounds of rending and tearing. "What did you do?" she whispered, and then louder as the cries were beginning to die down, "Damn you, *what did you do*?"

Jupiter glanced at her with open amusement. "My dear Screw," he said, "did you think that your precious and deceased partner was the only psionic in the world? Did you? There are more of us than you might think. Luta there . . . now she's quite good with mechanical things . . . that is, she has a positive knack for causing them to break down. Buzz there has a most uncanny way with animals. He can summon them and command them. Myself—I'm rather something of an odd case. What I do, you see, is shut down the powers of others if I so desire. Rather curious, don't you think?"

It was a bit much for Dakota to take in. She gestured toward Shai. "What about him?"

Shai chuckled. "I don't need no steenking powers," he said.

"Yes, we try to be patient with Shai," said Jupiter consolingly. "He can be rather devastating, but you know how it is with the slow ones. I assure you, we'll all grow on you."

"Like fungus."

He smiled thinly. "You still don't get it, do you? We're the good guys. We're the heroes."

She gave him as scathing a look as she could manage. "Then the good guys are pretty screwed up nowadays."

"You have absolutely no idea what we're trying to accomplish. No idea what's really going on out there. You have no comprehension of a world in which people who are concerned about the environment—people who want there to be something left for our children, people who care that the earth is being turned into a rotating cinder in space by a totalitarian government—people such as this, such as us, are outlaws. Villains."

"Murderers."

Jupiter suddenly shot forward, his hand lashing out and grabbing the front of Dakota's shirt. He pulled her close to him and hissed in her face, "The government is a murderer millions of times over. They murder nature. They murder people in the war effort. Who are we fighting? Who in hell are we fighting? No one is sure, but dammit, there's a war on. And we make weapons to fight in the war. Oh, heavens yes. Do you know what they were making in Internet Propulsion? Take a guess."

She tried to pull out of his grasp. "I don't know. Engines, I guess."

"Oh, yes. But their more popular product was chemicals used in chemical warfare. That used to be outlawed, did you know that? Before they repealed damn near all the rules of war since they were so afraid that hammerlocking weapons development would push our beloved governments into the only combat available, namely nuclear. Anything is better than nuclear, right? Devastate the people, the place, that's okay. But we have to keep the globe together for as long as it's possible to pick it clean."

Through gritted teeth she said, "If they were making chemicals and you blew the place up, you must have released some of it into the air. That wasn't exactly brilliant, now, was it?''

"They've already been dumping waste products into the water and air and ground. We're not happy about how we had to proceed, but at least we did something. And at least, for a while, that place won't spill out any more filth.''

He stared at her a moment longer, and seemed to be searching her eyes. "Am I getting through to you? Am I getting through at all?''

She merely returned his gaze levelly, silently. He shook his head sadly. "You know nothing,'' he said at length. Then he released her and stood, smoothing out his trousers. "All right. Let's get out of here.''

"And go where?'' said Shai. "It's the middle of the night.''

"If our location had been made, then we're sitting ducks here,'' Jupiter told him. "There's no point sitting around waiting for reinforcements to show up.''

"We have no transportation,'' Buzz pointed out.

"The soldiers who were all over us must have come in some sort of vehicles,'' Jupiter reasoned incorrectly. "Perhaps we can find one of theirs. Or perhaps this young lady here,'' and he pointed at Dakota, "will tell us where the vehicle she came in might be.''

"We got a flat,'' said Dakota.

"Hopefully, for your sake, you're lying,'' Jupiter said quietly.

"I'm not going,'' said Luta.

They all turned and looked at her. "Why on earth not?'' asked Jupiter.

"Because there's all kinds of creatures running around out there,'' she replied. "All those awful mutant things that Buzz called together.''

"Don't worry,'' said Buzz, getting to his feet and stretching. He tapped his forehead. "I can feel them all up here. As long as I got a brain in my head—and not a word out of you, Shai—I can control them. They won't harm us as long as I'm around."

"Asking a lot of faith here," rumbled Shai.

"I have faith in Buzz," Jupiter said calmly. "We are each of us experts, and if we don't respect each other's expertise, we really don't have much of anything, do we? So, gentlemen and ladies . . . let's get to it."

They made a practice of traveling light, so their few belongings were hastily shoved into backpacks and strapped on. Shai hauled Dakota to her feet and when she tried to stand she cried out. "Now what?" demanded Jupiter.

"I hurt my ankle," she said.

"Oh, really?" was his sarcastic reply. He grabbed the leg she was favoring and pulled it up to his eye level. Dakota staggered, Shai's firm grip preventing her from falling back. Jupiter rolled up her pants leg and yanked off her shoe and sock, and when he did Dakota let out a bloodcurdling scream.

In the woods nearby, Rommel's ears pricked up. A human had just screamed from somewhere close. Normally that would afford him little interest, for the general affairs of humans were of no consequence to him. But that voice sounded familiar, as if it might belong to the woman who traveled with them.

Even as the scream faded, Rommel was heading in the direction from which it had come.

"Oh, shit," said Luta.

She was reacting to Dakota's swollen ankle, red and angry. Even Shai winced slightly, and Jupiter was, if not sorry, at least a bit regretful.

"It appears you did indeed injure yourself," he admitted. "Very unfortunate. Shai, you'll have to carry her."

Dakota waited for some word of complaint or comment from the big man, but he said nothing. Instead he simply turned his broad back to her and indicated that she should climb on. It was not something she especially wanted to do, but she saw little choice. So on she climbed as Shai swung his backpack to his chest.

"All right," said Jupiter. "Let's go."

Buzz was in the lead as he confidently opened the door of the cabin and stepped out.

A gunshot cracked out.

Buzz staggered back, banging into Luta, who let out a shout of alarm. He spun, and Luta screamed as she saw the neat hole that had been drilled into Buzz's forehead. His eyes rolled up into the top of his head, and like a tree, he toppled forward and hit the floor.

Shai dropped to the floor, Dakota losing her grip and tumbling off his back. Luta was still screaming, gaze riveted to the blood that was beginning to stream down the sides of Buzz's head.

"The door!" shouted Jupiter. "Close the door!"

Shai's foot kicked out, hitting the door and slamming it shut. Over and over Luta was screaming, and Jupiter's shouts of "Shut up!" did nothing to stop her.

Buzz lay there, arms akimbo, blood and gore starting to puddle on the floor around him.

"Cover the window!" Jupiter ordered. "Quickly!"

"With what? Good intentions?" snapped back Shai.

They were all hugging the ground now, afraid to move. Jupiter felt a warmth around his fingers, realized that it was trickling over from Buzz and yanked his hand away.

"Oh God, oh God, oh God," Luta kept repeating. She had pulled her legs up and was rocking back and forth, sideways, her body trembling.

"Shut up!" he snapped, and had no more success with the order this time than he had earlier. "Shai . . . at least get the body out of here. Please."

Shai scrambled over to Buzz and, from a crouched position, picked him up. The back of his head stuck to the floor for a second but then came free, and without a word Shai tossed him out the window. Then he slid up the side of the wall next to the window, making sure not to present a target, reached over, and slid the window shut. "There," he said sarcastically. "Safe now."

"We're gonna die, we're gonna die," Luta was saying. Jupiter sighed—at least she had switched her hysteria to a different phrase.

"Will you please try to get a grip?" he said, averting his eyes from the puddle on the floor, which was all that remained of Buzz in the one-room cabin.

"Who did it?" said Shai.

"Had to be a soldier. Had to be," Jupiter reasoned, correctly this time. "Buzz's little friends didn't get everybody. Who knows how many more are out there."

"Hold on," said Shai. He had pulled out his automatic and scrabbled across the floor to the door.

"What the hell are you doing?" demanded Jupiter, and Shai ignored him as he opened the door a crack and slid his hand through. He fired off three quick shots and then slammed the door.

Dakota, who had been trying to recover her scattered wits, said, "What did you do that for?"

"To let them know we're armed," said Jupiter.

"And dangerous," Shai added.

"Looks to me like they're the ones who are more dangerous," Dakota observed.

In the darkness of the cabin, Jupiter said tightly, "I would be cautious about irritating us if I were you. How ever many of them are out there, they are obviously firing at the first thing to make itself a target. It would be very unfortunate for you if you happened to present a target, now, wouldn't it?"

Dakota, wisely, said nothing.

13

CHUCK'S LEGS WERE cramping up, his knees starting to become torn, and he was bleeding. It seemed that he couldn't remember the last time he had been warm and comfortable and not aching. He had developed a cough, a nasty-sounding one deep in his chest, and all around him the forest seemed alive. It *was* alive, as he heard rustling and shakings. He didn't know if something was stalking him, or if the leaves of trees were just blowing in stray winds. In the hidden recesses of his imagination, all sorts of hideous terrors lurked and strayed in his direction, claws extended and sharp teeth snapping.

He put his hand to his forehead. He felt hot to himself, which of course didn't mean anything. But it made him nervous as hell. Not only that, but his throat felt raw, partially from the coughing, partially from something else.

Chuck was not predisposed to getting sick. There was the old line about never being sick a day in your life. For Chuck that was pretty much true. His endurance and stamina were tremendous, and as for illness, he never suffered.

So why now? God help him, was it the river? Had trying to avoid drowning in the river only condemned him to something even worse?

He bent over, resting on all fours, listening to his breath rattle.

And then he jumped, startled, because of the huge crash off to his left. As if someone had dropped an anvil through the forest. His first thought was that some immense creature was coming at him, but the direction of it was odd. It really did sound like something coming down from overhead. A huge bird, maybe, shot down, except then he would have heard gunfire from nearby.

Then a brief, very human shriek and curses, getting progressively lower to the ground. Female—

A female had fallen from the sky.

Back in the day of being a feckless, horny teenage boy, he would have considered this a bounteous gift from God. Women from heaven. Maybe her name was Penny.

Now, though, he didn't know what to make of it. He tried to shout out, a cry of "I'm over here! Help me!" but nothing more than a mild croak emerged from his lips. He heard the rustling, and she sounded like she was only about twenty, thirty yards away, off to his left. But sounds were deceptive in the forest, he knew. Her voice might be bouncing off of trees. And for that matter, what was she doing here, anyway? He was assuming she was friend when she might be foe . . .

But what choice did he have? The blackness still hung over him, terrifying him. He felt as if his only chance for survival was connecting up with this woman, whoever she was. And he had to hope that she was better off at the moment than he was.

He stood up and moaned very softly, stretching his legs. His knees were a wreck—he couldn't possibly continue as he was. He was going to have to walk, as painful as that might be. He had to move quickly, because if he couldn't make his voice carry, he was going to have to find her before she vanished from the area.

The thought of moving away from the relative safety of the river edge, of plunging blindly into the forest, was horrifying. But Chuck took a deep breath, fought once again for the calm, clear center of his mind.

You didn't see simply with your eyes. When you were of a spiritual mind, he firmly believed, when you were one with nature, you shouldn't need to rely solely on your eyes. There had to be more. When he studied aikido, when he defended himself, and when he saw others in action, there was more than just sight involved. You defended yourself with a mind that sensed where blows were coming from, instinct that cued you to protect yourself. He had seen true aikido masters move so quickly, block and attack with such speed, that they were literally blurs.

There was sight. And then there was sight beyond sight.

So, the first step. Then the second. He started to move, leaving the river behind him. The sound of the rushing water had had a pacifying effect on him, as calming and nurturing as the sound of a mother's heart to a child in a womb. Now he was leaving the protection of that environment, of that sound.

He stopped dead. Something had warned him and he slowly reached out. Directly in his path, barely a few inches, was a tree.

Something had warned him. It wasn't just his psychic senses—those only seemed to react to the evil intent of people, and warn him of the danger they intended. A tree was neutral, not inherently dangerous or threatening. A tree was simply there.

His fingers passed over the trunk and he coughed. And smiled.

He stepped around the tree, feeling the first measure of confidence he had in quite some time.

And that was when he heard the roar that made his heart stop.

He jumped back, gasping. From ahead of him had been the sound of an animal, immense from the volume of it. Incredible sound, pure and savage, and hungry and angry—

And the woman.

"My God," he whispered, and he started to run. He wasn't

even thinking about it, even with the darkness hanging shroudlike over him. He ran, ran toward the sound that continued, growing louder and louder.

There was something crashing through the woods, coming toward him. He heard fast human gasps, female. It was the woman, somewhere there in the darkness of the forest and his mind.

And then something slammed into him, something soft yet hard. A woman, *the* woman, but her body was muscled and hard, and they went down in a tangle of arms and legs.

The blackness was unrelenting. He fought down panic, tried to calm himself, and then there was the roar, the *roar* from right in front of them.

"Run!" she shouted at him, which seemed very sound advice. He tried to clamber to his feet—

—and his feet left the ground.

The roar was absolutely deafening, was overwhelming, was everywhere. Something had grabbed him up, lifted him high into the air. He felt the claws raking across his arms, felt himself in the grip of something that could rip him apart. Indeed, was about to rip him apart.

How high was he? Five feet, ten, twenty? He'd lost all sense of distance, was totally out of control, had no idea what was up and down.

The darkness roared at him, blasting him with hot, fetid breath that nauseated him. He shoved back against something with his feet, knew he had planted them against a massive, hairy chest.

He was the pacifist, the lover of life. He had lost his temper once and unleashed the pure fury of his power and had sworn never to do so again. He had, indeed, feared this selfsame power for what it made him capable of, and had mentally placed his own psychic dampers on himself to contain his power. He had chained his power up to save lives.

And everywhere now, everywhere was the enraged bellowing of the animal, and the jaws were about to rip into his face, rip out his throat. No choice, no choice at all, and he cut free the chains and threw the dampers.

His mind lashed out, undisciplined, driven by panic, the power a tangible thing that ripped out at whatever it encountered and shredded it. It was as if he had vomited up a thunderbolt.

He had no idea what he had done, no clear vision of what he had accomplished. It had been a panicked, desperate move. All he knew was that the roaring had stopped, very, very suddenly, and he fell to the ground, no longer supported by whatever had been holding him.

He landed badly, one shoulder absorbing most of the impact, and he lay there, unable or afraid to move. He waited for the creature to attack again, for he was not positive what had just happened. His mind hazed and fogged over, and from a distance came a female voice saying something. But he couldn't make it out, couldn't understand a word.

He felt as if his entire body were on fire, and he coughed once hoarsely before letting the cool darkness claim him.

14

THE BEAR CHARGED at Jo Sanderson, and the sergeant ducked under the great sweeping paw, leaping and rolling to the side as fast as she could. Her gun was back in its holster, and even if she pulled it she was still out of ammo except for the half clip in her pocket. And even if she had a full magazine ready and loaded and fired every single round into the creature's chest from less than a foot away, the chances were that the thing would laugh it off before disemboweling her.

She scrambled to her feet and started to run. From right behind her came an enraged howl from the bear, and the sound of foliage crashing to the ground. It was right after her, moving with incredible speed, and she knew in her heart that there was absolutely no way she was doing anything other than prolonging the inevitable.

Her one and only chance was to make for the river that she had spotted as she had plummeted to the ground. But that was a long shot, and worse, it seemed likely that the animal would drive her to the ground before she got anywhere near the water. Worse, she wasn't even sure that she was heading in the right direction.

The bear was closing the gap, which hadn't been all that wide to start with. Her backpack jostled around and she considered trying to ditch it, but she would have had to slow down to do that. It didn't seem practical, or healthy, or indeed having much point at all.

And it was right after her as a swipe of its paw ripped through her backpack. It was that close, and it was about to be closer.

Jo put on an extra burst of speed, calling from the depths of herself, counting on every last bit of adrenaline that she could possibly summon. She dashed headlong through the woods—

—and crashed into a dark shape.

She knocked it flat and was tangled up with it, falling heels over head. In the darkness of the forest she could barely make it out—a mass of dark hair and a beard, it seemed, clothing ripped and shredded. Probably some sort of bum or derelict or Cutter who had chosen the woods as his home.

Wonderful. Now the woods were going to be his burial ground too, for the bear had caught up with them.

For all her desperation, and all her fury at this man who had accidentally blocked her path and guaranteed her death, she nevertheless had to do all she could to try to save one last life. "Run!" she shouted. She rolled to the side and, getting to her feet, began to wave madly as if signalling an airplane, trying to capture the beast's attention.

The beast didn't care. It was going to kill whatever it was looking at for the moment, and at the moment it was looking at the hapless forest dweller.

It grabbed the unfortunate man up, roaring in his face. The man was shoving his feet against the monster as if hoping to push it away. She couldn't make out his face in the darkness, but he was clearly terrified. Of course he was.

She knew it was hopeless, even pointless, but she couldn't stand by and do nothing. The bear was roaring even louder, as if announcing his intentions of killing the human it held in its grasp. Jo, in the meantime, yanked out her pistol, pulled the clip from her pocket. She slammed the clip home and brought it around, trying to find someplace she could aim at the bear that might have an effect. She wasn't a deadshot like Winkowski, but if she could drill the monster's eye . . .

The man was clearly at the end of his resistance, his body frozen, his back arching, his head trembling—

—and the bear exploded.

Sanderson's jaw dropped in disbelief. As if someone had shot a missile through it, all the major organs in the bear's chest exited out the creature's back with a sound like a volcano erupting. There was a perverse pattering sound, like rain, as vital liquids and organs showered down on the surrounding bushes and leaves. The bear staggered, confused, looking down as if noticing with great curiosity that someone had blown a hole in it the size of a sewer cover.

Its body refused to function, and the bear dropped the man and fell back, and then over, while uttering one last protest.

Sanderson stood frozen, staring from the man to the animal and back again, still not believing her eyes. The man lay there, moaning, and she went to him and took him by the shoulders. "Are you all right?" she said.

Closer to him now, her eyes becoming accustomed to the dark, she saw that he appeared to be an accident victim of some sort. His clothes were singed, his body was battered and bloody . . .

Could he have been caught in the explosion at the plant? But, no, that was impossible, certainly. There was no way he could have gotten from there to here unless . . .

He moaned, and when she touched his face she quickly withdrew her hand. "Lord, you're burning up," she whispered. "High fever. You look terrible. Who are you?"

He stared up at her, his eyes not appearing to focus on her face. There were more burns and singes around his eyes.

Suddenly a thought hit her, and she passed her hand in front of his face. He didn't react to it. "Can you see? Can you see me? Anything?"

His head lolled to the side, his eyes closed, and for a moment she was certain that he had just died. But no, he had simply passed out. From the sound of his breathing, though, it didn't sound any too likely that he was going to wake up. Still, she couldn't just leave the guy here. For chrissakes, she owed him her life.

Didn't she? What in hell had just happened here, anyway? That monstrous animal—and she glanced in the direction of the shattered corpse—had been about to make a late-night snack out of him, and then suddenly had blown to pieces as if someone had dropped a grenade down its throat. But how had that happened? Had he been packing a weapon of some sort? She checked him over quickly, but found no weapons. No ID either. He must have dropped it somewhere along the way . . .

The way from where?

Who *was* this guy?

She had to get back to her men. But by the same token, again, she wasn't going to leave this stranger in the middle of the woods.

Jo pulled out her compass to verify her direction. Her main hope was to make it through the woods, find a passage that would bring her back up the cliffs and rejoin her squad—what was left of it—in time to prevent the Extremists who had blown up the plant from escaping.

She blew air through her lips. Right. That was all she had to do. Oh, and do it while lugging this guy. For she knew that that was her only option.

She lifted him up. He was heavy, but nothing she couldn't handle. If there was one thing that Jo Sanderson was confident in, it was her strength. Maybe she was no match for one-on-one with the grizzly from hell, but she could haul this guy around, no problem.

She swung him around so that his left arm was around her shoulder, and she supported the rest of him with her right. She hoped that this would bring him around faster, although with the way he was feeling, she wasn't holding out hope.

She started walking, and she whispered to him, "Come on, keep the feet moving, left, left, left raht left . . ."

Through cracked and dry lips he muttered something faintly. A name. Maybe the name of a loved one. She listened closely and made out, in a faint whisper, "Rommel."

She shook her head.

Who was this guy?

15

WINKOWSKI LAY IN the bushes and wondered how much longer he had to live.

The young soldier had gotten over the initial panicked drive that had seized hold of him when they had been besieged by those mutant animals. Yes, gotten over it . . . but not before he had run like mad, putting as much distance between himself and that orgy of hysteria as possible.

He clutched his handgun, his only weapon, and peered through the bushes once more. It was still dark, but he could see the outline of the cabin in front of him. His eyes, he had always boasted, were the sharpest in the squad. Maybe in the army. It made him terribly effective at night, and also the best shot in the outfit.

It had also enabled him, miraculously, to carry the fight to the enemy.

Claude Winkowski had never shot anyone before.

He had been in training, had even been on maneuvers. He had even participated in a police action, overrunning some Fifth World Nation. But everyone there had practically surrendered on sight, and hardly any shots were fired. Certainly none by him, at any rate.

He almost felt self-conscious about it. He had also wondered when and if the time came, whether he would be able to do it. For Winkowski had always had doubts about his ability as a soldier. His marksmanship was unparalleled—the squad nickname for him was Hawkeye. But that was simply a skill. Everyone had skills. He wasn't sure whether he had the spirit, the guts, the *do you have what it takes* sort of stuff.

And his general sense of concern was not aided by the fact that he had run when shit had gone down. He tried to tell himself that it was understandable, that it wasn't his fault. That he had spent his time preparing to fight human enemies, not bizarre mutants. That if he had stayed, fought, he probably would have died along with most of his squad. Maybe all, because he hadn't seen anyone else. He tried to tell himself so many things, but all of them boiled down to the fact that he had run, goddammit, he had run.

He had to make up for it somehow.

Luck had been with him, however, in the direction that he had run. For it had taken him straight through the brush to within sight of a cabin. His eyes had widened as he had seen, parked outside the cabin, a very familiar van. A gray van with a crunch in the fender off of which Dorsch had been hurled earlier in this hellish evening.

The van belonged to the Extremists, and it was parked in front of the cabin. Therefore, (elementary logic dictated) the Extremists were inside the cabin. And he was outside the cabin. That realization was quickly followed by another— he knew they were in there, but they didn't know he was out here. If he could stay out of sight, hold them there until reinforcements showed up . . .

God, how would they know? How would they know where he was?

He scratched his head and suddenly felt like a major fool. His comm unit was on his belt, right where it should be. He could try and get in touch with someone, tell them where he was, summon help . . .

He paused, holding his breath.

There had definitely been some sort of movement within

the cabin. And now the front door was opening and a man was framed in the doorway. He was tall, fuzzy, scuzzy . . .

Winkowski's eyes widened. He recognized him instantly. His eyes—his wonderful, magnificent, sharp eyes—had seen that figure behind the wheel of the van that struck Dorsch. This was him, this was the bastard who had steamrolled right over one of his best buddies.

The action was immediate, the mechanics smooth because of long practice. He brought the gun up, aimed, and squeezed off a shot all in just over a second.

The bullet drilled the bastard in the forehead. He staggered back, his eyes sweeping the woods as if trying to spot where the bullet had come from, but actually it was just reflex. The brain was already dead, Winkowski was certain.

He tumbled back into the darkness of the cabin, and there was a satisfying chorus of shouts. Everyone from inside was yelling at once, and a woman had screamed and another woman was saying something repeatedly, and then the door slammed shut.

A cold, hard smile of satisfaction split Winkowski's face. He'd done it. Chalk up one for the good guys.

The door opened slightly and several shots spit out from a gun. None came remotely near Winkowski. They were blind shots. They had no idea where he was, no idea how many soldiers surrounded the cabin. It was just exactly what he wanted and how he wanted it to be.

He sat there, wondering what to do next. From his angle he could see both the front door and the side window. He hoped there wasn't a back, or they could escape out the back and he'd never spot them.

Suddenly there was a movement at the side window. He started to respond, shift his position, when that movement abruptly produced a body. It was the man he'd shot and killed, and he was being unceremoniously tossed out the most convenient aperture. It indicated that there was no back door, otherwise they would most certainly have used that.

Winkowski watched him sail into the bushes with cold pleasure. And it was then, and only then, that a truth began to settle in. He had killed someone. He had actually used his skill, the God-given skill of the hawk's eye, and had exercised the life of a human. Like a surgeon, cutting out a cancer with a scalpel.

He shouldn't feel bad about it, after all. He knew that, was certain of it beyond all doubt. This guy, whoever he was, had been responsible for killing Dorsch. Had been responsible, at least partially, for blowing up a government installation. Had been responsible for death, destruction, and mayhem.

And somewhere, somehow . . .

Sometime in the past . . .

Had been a teenager, discovering his first kiss, having sex for the first time. Had been a child, running and playing, dreaming about being an astronaut or doctor or maybe even a soldier. Had been a baby, brought into the world, crying and squalling, cradled and nursed and, hopefully, loved.

All those experiences, all those things that Claude Winkowski had been through as well.

The guy had killed Dorsch. Winkowski had killed him. Simple as that.

He could see the man's—the corpse's—foot sticking out from the underbrush. The foot of the man, the teen, the child, and the babe, and that life had been taken away by one squeeze of one trigger. Something ephemeral and irreplaceable, gone.

Winkowski felt tears rolling down his cheeks and furiously wiped them away. Finally he'd gotten his first blood, and this was how he was reacting? God, and he called himself a soldier.

A sudden movement off to the left brought his attention around.

The glowing eyes of an animal stared at him from out of the underbrush. He could barely make it out, but even in shadow he could see that the thing was huge. Monstrous. Probably another mutant.

He didn't want to start firing. It was vital that he preserve ammo, because he didn't know for sure how many people were in the cabin. If he wound up getting in a firefight, he needed enough ammunition—not to mention plain old luck—to survive. Besides, if he started firing, it might give away his position.

He took dead aim on the animal, still hidden in the shadows of the underbrush. It wasn't moving. Winkowski wasn't even sure it was especially interested in him.

"Get out of here," hissed Winkowski.

The animal seemed to hesitate a moment . . . and then it vanished back into the undergrowth.

Winkowski was amazed. He couldn't believe his good fortune. Had he gotten through to the creature? Was it actually afraid of him? Maybe it just wasn't hungry—having sated itself, he realized in grisly fashion, on the bodies of other soldiers.

Whatever the reason, the animal had moved off, and Winkowski was not about to knock it.

He settled back to wait for further developments, and tried not to think about the body that was lying unmoving in the bushes.

Rommel tried to figure out what to do.

He walked the perimeter of the cabin area, sleekly and silently, and picked up the scent of the woman, Dakota. There were others with her. There was also some idiot hiding in the bushes with a gun, one of those who was dressed like the ones from the place where Chuck and he had first met. Now what was the name for those creatures again? Oh, yes . . . Chuck had called them *soldiers*.

Well, this soldier had seemed less than impressive. His face had been wet and his hand trembling as he had held a gun on Rommel and stammered at him. Rommel considered attacking him but saw nothing to gain. He wasn't going to eat him, and aside from the fact that the soldier was pointing a gun at him, there was no threat.

Rommel hadn't eaten in some time, hadn't slept, and he was starting to get a little worn down. If an argument could be avoided, by all means Rommel decided to avoid it. Besides, the man wasn't what was making him nervous.

It was the other dog.

There had been several rather vicious and curious animals in the area, but they seemed to have wandered off, as if they'd lost their purpose. But there was still a dog around. It was in the cabin, and it had marked the perimeter with its scent. It was a big one, from the smell of it. Big and nasty, and it had probably eaten.

Chuck, where are you? demanded Rommel.

The comm unit on Winkowski's belt crackled to life. He removed it and spoke in a low, hurried voice. "Pigeon Six here," he whispered.

"Thank God," came the reply.

"Panther Six?" He couldn't believe it. Jo Sanderson had always treated him well, always seemed ready and willing to listen to him. He had privately begun mourning her, and could barely contain his excitement. "Panther Six, is that you?"

"Yes. I can barely hear you."

"I'm whispering. I'm keeping surveillance on the cabin where the Extremists are. I've already taken down one of them."

There was a pause on the other end. "Is that confirmed?"

"He's dead, Panther Six. I made sure of that."

Another brief pause, and then she said, "Are you okay?"

The question held more than the surface meaning, and he knew it, and it was only one of the many reasons that he was devoted to her. "Fine, Panther Six."

"Keep an eye on them. Do nothing to make yourself a

target, understand? I've lost enough men on this debacle, I don't want to lose you, too.''

"I've no intention of getting lost, Panther Six. Where are you?"

"Believe it or not, just outside of a cabin."

Surprised, he looked around, scanning the perimeter as best he could. "I don't see you."

"That's because I'm nowhere near your position. I'm at another cabin. Some abandoned, run-down thing."

"You sure it's a different one? Maybe the Extremists are inside."

"Well, I've just entered, and I don't see anyone else here. I'll be there as soon as I can. Panther Six over."

"Over and under, Panther Six."

Winkowski slipped the comm link back onto his belt, and then settled back to keep watch. He stayed absolutely still, because for all he knew one or more of those mutant creatures was still wandering around in the neighborhood, and he didn't want to do anything that might encourage them to come over and visit.

16

Jo Sanderson closed her comm unit and turned back to her rather curious patient.

He lay sprawled on one of three tattered-looking bedrolls spread on the floor. He was on his back, his chest rising and falling slowly and irregularly. Every so often he would cough, a nasty-sounding rattle that didn't bode well.

She had no idea who owned the cabin, or if anybody did. It was hard to tell how long the bedrolls had been lying there—maybe days, maybe months. Impossible to tell considering how filthy they were. But they were better than nothing. Indeed, the whole cabin definitely fell into the realm of "better than nothing," but when Jo had spotted it, she couldn't believe her good fortune. Her shoulders and legs were becoming sore at the weight of the bearded stranger, and when the light from her flashlight had picked up the cabin, she had been thrilled.

It had not stopped her from proceeding with care, of course. She had peered cautiously through the windows before entering, wanting to make sure that she wasn't just barging in on someone. Not that she cared particularly if she was disturbing an occupant or rousing them from their slumber. But if someone were already there and they were armed, it could get sticky. Fortunately, whoever had been occupying the cabin had apparently departed ages ago.

The door had been unlocked, so entry had been easy. And moments later she had the mysterious man lying on one of the dirty bedrolls, looking very flushed in the glow of her flashlight.

After Jo had finished her conversation with Winkowski, she tore a narrow strip of cloth from the end of one of the sleeping bags and wet it with water from her canteen. Then she applied the compress across his forehead. He moaned softly, and he was still hot and shivering.

"Can you hear me?" she asked him softly.

There was no response from him, no sign that he had heard her. But he had stopped coughing, and that certainly had to be a good sign.

Jo was no doctor. Her mother had been a registered nurse, and that gave her some feeling for what she should be doing. But, dammit, she realized that what she should be doing is getting back to her squad, not screwing around with this guy. So he was sick. So what? There were plenty of sick people in the world. So he had saved her life—

Had he? Was he really responsible for stopping the creature, or had something about that monster's nature just caused it to—to what? Spontaneously disintegrate? Was it possible? Hell, sure it was possible. After all, she was thinking about a creature that by rights shouldn't even exist in nature. Anything was possible.

So all right. So now what?

He shivered, and she pulled another sleeping bag over him, trying to provide him with additional warmth. She removed the compress and placed her hand against his cheek. Already he seemed cooler from it, and she raised an eyebrow. "Whatever you've got, you seem to be a fast healer, guy."

He moaned softly, and again muttered the name "Rommel."

She frowned at that. Now why in the world would he care about Field Marshal Rommel? Was he a history buff or something?

Jo rose and stretched her legs, glancing around the cabin to see if there was anything else that could be of some use. It didn't appear so. A table, a few chairs and other sticks of furniture, some empty tins of food. Nothing much that gave her anything to work with.

Her mysterious patient moaned more loudly this time. He seemed to be dreaming, twisting in his sleep and muttering. She bent over him, trying to make out what he was saying.

It sounded like names of places. He said what sounded like North Dakota, and then started muttering something that sounded like "Butte, tell Butte," and she wasn't sure what the hell Butte, Montana had to do with anything.

He started to shake and tremble, sweating even more. She reapplied the compress, shaking her head, and then he said, "Complex."

That made her ears prick up. Could he simply be using the conventional word? But it was an odd thing to say. Or could he be referring to that mysterious and powerful agency that lived a shadowy existence and was, by all accounts, practically omniscient? Was this guy an agent of the Complex? Or maybe the Complex was after him?

Now that put an interesting spin on things. If the Complex was after this guy and she was aiding him, wasn't that leaving her open for criminal charges?

A lot of "ifs." A lot of supposition. And she owed him her life . . . didn't she?

He cried out, arching his back. She looked down, unsure of what to do. "Shhh," she said. "It's okay. You're safe." But whatever dream world he was in wasn't letting him go quite that easily.

And suddenly the food tins rose into the air.

Jo didn't notice them at first, so distracted was she with the writhings of her patient. But then she did spot them and her eyes widened. "What the hell . . . ?" she whispered.

"Get away from me!" he shouted into the air. His eyes snapped open but he didn't seem to see anything. Or else whatever he was seeing was in his mind. "Get away! Get away!"

Jo suddenly screamed as she was yanked off her feet.

She sailed across the room, totally out of control, as if in the grip of an overwhelming power. Nearby the furniture rose up, and a chair hurtled across the room in her direction. In midair she nevertheless managed to twist so that the chair just missed her, crashing against the wall behind her.

Jo shrieked, not believing what was happening. Everything in the room had gone berserk, flying into the air and whirling about as if caught in an invisible maelstrom. The man rolled over, gasping, crying out, and Jo slammed up against the ceiling, crushed against it, and feeling massive, unseen power shoving her hard against it. She thought her ribs were going to crack, fancied that her lungs were collapsing.

"Stop it!" she screamed. "Stop it!"

She started to descend and then was slammed harder against the ceiling, spread-eagled against it. Things were hurtling everywhere. The table shattered under the pressure, rotting wood collapsing. A window blew out in an explosion of timber and glass. The door was blasted open on its hinges, and in the center of all the tumult, of all the insanity, was the dreaming man on the floor. The very air around her seemed alive, roaring in fury, as if a storm had moved into the center of the cabin.

Jo's fingers clawed toward her holstered gun. She didn't want to do it, but there was no choice. She felt the pressure increasing against her and she cried out, certain that she had waited too long. Certain she was going to die, pulped by this bizarre individual who could kill even in his dreams.

She managed to pull the gun from its holster and she brought the weapon around, aiming it dead center at the dreamer.

And suddenly she fell to the floor.

Just like that, whatever was going through the mind of the tortured dreamer ended. Jo landed with a thud and rolled, coming quickly up to a defensive stance, her gun held out in front of her in a two-handed grip. She was gasping for breath, her short blond hair disheveled, her eyes wild. It was the second time in this insane evening that she'd been airborne, out of control, and it was definitely not one of her favorite habits.

The man lay there, gasping for breath, still very obviously asleep. Jo backed against the wall, trying to get as far from him as possible, her eyes and gun not leaving him for a second.

She had heard whispered rumors about people like him. She'd never witnessed it, to some degree never seen it before. *Psionic.*

"Gotta get out of here," she muttered. She had no business hanging out anyway. She was in a cabin with someone who could rip her to shreds just by having a bad dream. Sure, he had obviously saved her life. So what? He'd been busy saving his own. She had just been along for the ride.

Part of her warned her that she should shoot him anyway, just to be safe. Who knew how far his power extended? But she couldn't do it. But what she could do was get the hell out of the cabin.

Which was exactly what she did.

17

THE EXTREMISTS HAD been lying on the floor of the cabin, unmoving and unspeaking, for quite some time. Dakota couldn't help but observe that it was as if they were in shock, unable to accept what happened. Unable to believe that, whatever their plans were, they had gone so wrong.

"Porky, and now Buzz," said Luta softly. "They're getting us all, Jupiter. We're all going to die. Why are we doing this? Why?"

Jupiter remained silent, and it was Shai who said, "Because it's what we have to do. Because we see what's happening and we can't turn away."

Dakota thought that bleakly amusing. That was the sort of claptrap she always heard Chuck spouting. But these guys, who used violence to suit their needs, sure as hell weren't members of the Society of Friends. "You mean you don't thrill to a life of danger?" said Dakota.

From the darkness, Shai said, "Would you like to know just how much you know?"

"I really don't care."

"My son died at age three. His lungs never developed the ability to breathe the crap that passes for our air. My wife died two years after that. Skin cancer, because the ozone layer has deteriorated so badly that the sun's rays are our enemy."

"There are ozone factories—" she began.

"Uh-huh. And why do you think there are? Because people like us spread the word about what was happening. If we hadn't, nothing would have been done. As it is, it's probably too little, too late."

He was silent for a time after that, and then Dakota said quietly, "I'm sorry about your family."

He didn't respond.

"Are we all enjoying being maudlin?" said Jupiter. "Or should we be considering methods of getting out of here?"

"Like what?" said Luta. "If any of us stick our heads out, we'll be shot. There could be a dozen guys out there."

"Then why don't they attack already?" said Jupiter.

"Because they don't know how many of us there are, or what our weapons are," said Shai. "And why should they? They can just wait until reinforcements show up. Or they could wait until a bomber shows up and we can just be bombed out of existence. So why should they risk their necks?"

"So that's it," said Luta. "We go out, we get shot. And even if we don't get shot, there's still animals running around. You know, the creatures that Bu—Buzz summoned. Lurking about somewhere, and they'll attack us because Buzz isn't here."

"That's very possible," agreed Jupiter.

"So what do we *do*?" wailed Luta. "I can't put their weapons out of commission while they're hidden. I can only affect what I see. And if we come out they'll shoot us."

"We could pretend to surrender, and when they come out, you could short-circuit them," said Jupiter, thinking out loud. But then he frowned. "But if I were them, I'd hold a few men in hiding, just in case. Even one hidden marksman could still pick us off. Damn, if only we knew how many were out there."

And Shai said quietly, "If this is our time to die, then we die. With honor. With dignity. With the same sort of honor and dignity that we wish man gave to the planet that birthed him. We have to provide an example.''

''I don't want to provide an example,'' said Luta. ''I want to see my birthday next week.''

Shai glanced at her. ''Next week's your birthday?''

''Tuesday.''

''In case we're dead by then, happy birthday.'' And Shai laughed low in his throat.

''Jupiter! Make him stop that! Make him stop saying that!''

Jupiter gave Shai a pleading look, and Shai smiled to himself but said nothing further.

''Now . . .'' Jupiter said after a moment of thought, ''we will be able to get out of this.''

Luta sat up anxiously. ''How? How?''

''Our bargaining chip.'' And he inclined his head in Dakota's direction.

''No way,'' said Dakota tightly. ''You do whatever you damned want, but leave me out of it.''

''I'm sorry you feel that way. Mars . . .''

The dog, whom Dakota had almost forgotten about, stood up obediently in the darkened corner.

Jupiter pointed at Dakota. ''Kill.''

The dog charged at Dakota. She screamed, throwing her arm up in hopeless self-defense as the Doberman closed on her, jaws snapping. But just before the jaws could clamp down, Jupiter's stern voice said, ''Stop.''

Mars halted, inches short of Dakota, and swiveled his large head. He growled, and Dakota was reminded of Rommel and Chuck's holding him back from killing that Cutter. She prayed that Jupiter's command over Mars was as strong.

''Heel, Mars. Good dog.'' Jupiter spoke in a no-nonsense tone, and Mars obediently backed away from Dakota. But he never took his eyes from her.

Dakota slowly let out her breath. From nearby, Shai said sternly, ''That wasn't nice, Jupe.''

Jupiter looked at him incredulously. ''Being pinned down

by the military must be mucking with your memory, Shai. I never claimed to be a nice person. Now, my dear Screw, you will do exactly as I say or next time I don't hold Mars off. Is that understood?'' She nodded. "Now . . . what is your name?''

"Bailey.''

"Bailey,'' he repeated. "And your first name?''

"Barnum N.''

He smiled in that lipless way he had. "Droll. Very droll. All right then, Screw, now listen carefully. Your life will depend on it.''

Hidden in the bushes, unmoving for what seemed forever, Winkowski carefully straightened out his cramping leg. His nerves were shot, being as high-keyed for so long a time as they were. Every so often he had to shake his hand briskly to restore circulation, since he was keeping his finger wrapped around the trigger for so long a time.

He saw no need to clutter up the airwaves by constantly contacting the sergeant. The sarge certainly sounded as if she had the situation in control, and besides, he didn't want to make any unnecessary noise. He had had one more communication with her after the first one—she had sounded out of breath, like she was running. She also sounded very jumpy, as if she had just been through a very jolting or disturbing experience. Well, certainly she had. They all had been. He had reconfirmed his position, and she had told him she was on her way. She had even, she said, spotted what appeared to be a passage that would bring her up and around the cliffs.

He glanced at his watch. The sun would be coming up in a few hours . . . not that anyone saw the sun much these days, but at least it was comforting to know that it was there.

He heard the door of the cabin creak and immediately brought his gun up, sighting carefully. Something poked through the door, and he blinked in surprise—a flag. No, not a flag—a piece of cloth, but it was definitely white.

Were they surrendering? He couldn't believe it. Then he had a flash of panic. What if they were? He couldn't just shoot people who were giving up. But if they gave up, he'd have to reveal that it was just him. If only he knew how many of them there were. If only he had heavy armaments that he could use to just blow up the whole cabin. Just a few shells from an RBG, or even a grenade or two.

The door opened a bit wider, and a woman appeared. Her hands were behind her back, and the rope wrapped around her stomach indicated the hands were tied. She looked disheveled and frightened, but was clearly trying to keep up a brave front.

Winkowski lowered his gun slowly, uncertain of how to proceed. Was this legitimate? Was it bullshit? What was going down here? He wished desperately that a CO were on hand. Planning, strategy, decision making—these had never been his strengths. Point, aim, fire—these were what made up his life.

From inside a voice called out, "Army people . . . listen carefully. We have what you folks are so fond of calling a 'situation' on our hands. The young lady whom you see in the doorway is an agent of the Complex. As such, she has some value to you, I would think."

Winkowski's eyes widened. Christ almighty, the Complex. Were they lying? Maybe she was one of the Extremists. But what if they weren't lying.

"We've already killed her partner," the voice continued. "We will kill her if we are driven to it. We would prefer not to. But we will require safe passage if this agent is to continue to live."

The young soldier said nothing. To call out would be to give his position away. He knew they had firearms. The question was how many, and even more, how many were aimed at the woods. He had to proceed very, very carefully.

"By no later than what you would call oh-nine-hundred hours, we want to have a helicopter to take us to the nearest airport," called the voice, "and from there, passage to Mexico. The agent will stay with us until such time that we are clear. After that, she will be released. Make no mistake—we are prepared to die if we have to. And if you are interested in capturing a house full of corpses, feel free to wait until one minute after oh-nine-hundred. We will not be taken alive . . . but neither will she."

The young woman was yanked from view, and the door slammed shut. Winkowski let out a long, slow breath. This was definitely not good—not good at all.

He'd wait for the sarge to get here, but he was going to have to let her know, soon, just what was going on. He was going to need orders and strategy. And he was going to need them fast.

18

THE FIRST THING that Chuck slowly became aware of was the odd fabric beneath his hand. It was resting on something coarse and dirty. His hand moved over and touched bare floor.

He was inside somewhere. Well, that was an improvement.

He tried to remember what had happened to him. He seemed to recall a woman, and some sort of roaring creature. He remembered very little else, his thoughts being as scrambled as they were. And . . . he had killed. That was it. His TK had lashed out, as if it had a life of its own, and destroyed in some way the creature that had wanted to kill him. More blood on Chuck's hands.

Slowly he sat up, taking a deep breath and then letting it out. There was no raspiness, much to his surprise, and he repeated the cleansing breath. Whatever had been in his lungs had worked itself out.

All was still darkness, though. He passed his hand in front of a shadow. But it was hard to be sure whether it was really there, or whether he just so *wanted* it to be that he was imagining it.

Slowly he got to his feet, trying to deal with the concept of the blackness. He put his hands out to his side, then in front of him, and started to walk forward very slowly and carefully. He tried to reach out, get a feeling of his surroundings. Each step was tentative, for he still had no idea what might await him. And then he stopped in his tracks, reached forward, and touched the wall.

He smiled. He had sensed it there, just as he had sensed the tree. Maybe he was going to be able to do this after all.

And suddenly he heard the sounds of footsteps. There had to be a porch or something of some kind, because it was definitely feet on wood. There was nowhere he could hide, and even if there were, he couldn't see it.

He faced where he thought the door was, arms hanging loosely at his sides, and waited. The door creaked open, and in his darkness, Chuck faced the newcomers. He put up his hands and said, "Don't be alarmed. I've . . . been in an accident. It's damaged my sight somewhat, and made me a little ill. I'm not even sure how I wound up here, but I assure you that—"

And from the blackness of Chuck's world, a voice said, "I don't believe it."

His blood chilled. He knew that voice.

"That's him, isn't it? That's the bastard that landed Mort in the hospital!"

Chuck was truly impressed. It wasn't often that someone could be in a near-fatal explosion, be burned up, be blinded, be sick—and *then* have things go wrong. All in one night. Well, the up side was that, at this rate, he wasn't going to have to worry about the next night.

"You're the Cutters," he said tonelessly. "The ones from the diner."

"Two out of three of us. You and your damned monster almost killed Morrie."

" 'Morrie' would be dead if it weren't for me," said Chuck, but he didn't think his argument was going to hold much weight. Even as he spoke, his mind raced ahead trying to anticipate the situation.

They'd kill him, or try to. That much was plain, even to a blind man.

He had to do something. He lashed out with the power of

his mind in defense, driving it with the primitive need to survive. And he heard an explosion of timber, and the men shouted and gasped. Chuck didn't know what had just happened, but one of the Cutters inadvertently filled him in as he shouted, ''The table just blew up! How the hell did that happen?!''

Chuck was less than thrilled. He had no real ability to control his power, not without sight. He could try to lift them up, hurl them out, but he might wind up crushing them, or blowing them to pieces. He would not, could not take that risk. Even if it meant his own life.

But it didn't have to. From long practice, he dropped into his defensive aikido position, arms and legs poised. His breathing was slow, measured, and controlled.

They were there, somewhere in the darkness. He knew they would come at him. He tried to reach out, feel them with his mind. He listened with his ears, sensed with his nose. Tried to hear the sound of their feet coming at him.

There was a quick scuffle from his right. He turned, ready to meet it—

—and he was grabbed from behind. It had come from nowhere, startled him, frightened him. For a moment he lost his balance and concentration, considered switching to his psi power now that a foe was in proximity. But what if he overapplied it?

Moves that should have come instinctively, thoughts that should have flowed in orderly fashion, were scrambled and uncertain. Before he could make any move at all, a meaty fist slammed into his stomach. He gasped, gagged, his head spinning. Another blow from the darkness, this one to his face, and his head snapped around. He tasted his own blood, welling up from a split lip.

The man was still holding him from the back. Dammit, this should be easy, automatic. But everything seemed to be coming from everywhere, simultaneously. He twisted, tossed the man to the ground, but then Chuck's feet were knocked out from under him and he crashed to the floor. He tried to stand up, tried to get to his feet, but a booted foot kicked him in the stomach. There had been a quick whistling of air as it had approached, he realized, but too late. Too late. It knocked the wind out of him, and another kick to the side knocked him over. He tried to roll and keep rolling, but he crashed up against a wall.

Using the wall for support, he tried to pull himself up. Something, heaven knew what, warned him, and he dodged a furious punch aimed right at his head. He grabbed the wrist while still at full extension and yanked down, driving a knee upward and toward the pit of his attacker's stomach. It was not the kind of move he usually made, but one of desperation. It showed, because it was poorly executed and wound up glancing off the man's leg.

Something grabbed him from nowhere and hurled him to the ground, and the punches and kicks started coming. They seemed to be everywhere. It was as if a hundred men were in the room, each with a dozen arms, all attacking simultaneously. He cried out, bringing his arms up in front of his face to avoid a kick in his teeth, bringing his knees up to guard his vitals. And they wouldn't let up, pounding him, hurting him.

He felt the power welling up in him. *Kill them,* it whispered, *kill them. You don't have to take this abuse.*

"N-no," he choked out, and they thought he was talking to them. They laughed harshly, and Chuck could hear one of them drawing back his foot to kick him again, but he couldn't tell where it was coming from. He had completely lost balance, lost touch with the world and himself.

And then a hammer was cocked.

He was certain it was a gun aimed at him until a crisp female voice said, "Back away from him."

There was the sound of choked disbelief from the Cutters. "I mean it. Back away from him. Now."

The voice was new to Chuck, and yet somehow vaguely familiar. He heard his assailants sputter in indignation, saying, "He was trespassing! This is our place! We found it first! There's our sleeping stuff, right there!"

"And that gives you the right to beat him to death."

"What gives you the right to say we can't? That thing probably isn't even loaded."

There was the sound of a gunshot and a stifled shriek from the Cutters.

"There are three choices," she said. "You get out of here. Or get it in the heart. Or get it in the balls. The first option is yours. The second two will be mine, and you can't be sure which I'll pick."

There was the quick, hurried shuffling of feet, and within moments they were receding into the woods.

Chuck lay there, trying not to moan, and only partly succeeding. Then a soft voice, the woman's, said, "You okay?"

"Ohhhhh . . . fine," said Chuck, trying to sound jovial. He spit out a wad of what he suspected was blood. At least it wasn't a tooth. "We were . . . discussing religion . . . or politics. One of those. You know how . . . nasty those arguments can get . . ."

He tried to sit up and gasped. Then she was at his side, helping him. "Don't do it if you feel you're going to hurt something."

"No, I'll be fine. Really," he said. "I learned . . . how to roll with punches."

"Obviously." She felt his forehead. "You're cool. That's impressive. A few hours ago you were white-hot."

"I've always been a quick healer," he said, and then paused. "You were here before." It wasn't a question.

"You remember?"

"Not very much. Some." He took a deep breath and was pleased at the lack of pain and raspiness. Not only was whatever in his chest gone, but apparently he'd been lucky enough to avoid cracked ribs from the pounding he'd taken. "How do I look?"

"You're going to have some nasty bruises. At least one black eye. Can't be sure about the other stuff."

"Who are you?"

"Sergeant Mary Jo Sanderson."

"Police?"

"Army."

"Oh," he said.

"And you are—?"

"Chuck Smith." He hated lying, especially to someone who had saved his life. But he had no choice, especially with her being attached to the government. For all he knew she had standing orders to shoot Chuck Simon on sight.

She helped him over to the sleeping bags and lay him down. "You were here earlier?" he said.

"Yeah."

"Don't take this wrong, but why'd you leave? And why'd you come back?"

There was a long pause, and he sensed that whatever answer he was going to get wasn't going to be the whole truth. As if they were playing a waiting game, waiting for the other one to be fully honest and neither was willing to do so first.

"I felt I owed it to you to come back," she said after a time. "To make sure you were okay."

"And why'd you leave?"

An even longer pause. "Something came up," she said finally, and from the finality of her tone it was clear that she wasn't about to elaborate on that. "Here . . . have some water."

He hesitated. "Where'd the water come from?"

"It's in my canteen. Filled it at base."

"Not from the local water?"

She uttered an unfunny laugh. "You're kidding, right?"

She brought the canteen up to his lips and he gulped down the water greedily. She had to pull it away from him when he started to choke. "You shouldn't laugh about the native water," he said.

"What're you, an environmental Extremist or something?"

The question was very carefully phrased and Chuck hesitated. She sounded suspicious of something. "No. Just someone in the wrong place at the wrong time. Someone who took an extended swim in the river out there. I think that's what made me sick."

"If that's the case, you were damned lucky you recovered at all," she said.

"You're not kidding."

There was a pause as she said, "I'm going to have to get going soon. You . . . can't see, can you?"

"Not at the moment," he admitted. "I'm hoping it clears up."

"Then maybe you'd better—"

There was a beep from nearby and he turned his head in confusion, wondering what had caused it. "My comm unit," Jo told him upon seeing his puzzlement. She clicked it on and said, "Go ahead."

"This is Pigeon Six," a nervous voice came over. "Sorry to bother you, Panther Six. Are you on the move?"

"Very shortly. What's the problem? Are they trying to get out?"

"They've got a hostage."

"Tough shit."

"They said she's with the Complex."

That gave her pause. "That could be a problem. If it's true."

"They said they killed her partner and are ready to kill her if we don't provide them means of escape."

Chuck sat up upon hearing this. His head hurt when he did it, but he brushed the pain aside. "What does the woman look like?" he said. "Did he see her? Ask him what—"

"Pigeon Six, can you describe her?" asked Jo.

"About medium height, long brown hair. Kind of pretty. Wearing jeans, red flannel shirt, black t-shirt under it—"

"Oh, God," said Chuck. "Oh, God, it's Dakota."

"Didn't copy that?" Winkowski said over the comm unit.

"Stand by, Pigeon Six." She snapped shut the comm unit and said to Chuck, "Level with me. Is she with the Complex? Are you?"

He didn't want to lie to her, but he had heard the flat, impersonal reply she had given when she had first thought that there was simply a civilian held hostage. So instead he said carefully, "You have to understand . . . even if we were with the Complex, I couldn't tell you."

"It would explain a hell of a lot," she said softly. She clicked back on the comm unit. "Pigeon Six, keep a lid on there. How long do we have?"

"Deadline is oh-nine-hundred."

"Okay, look. Use the alternate frequency and, very quietly, try to raise somebody. A troop should be arriving soon to launch a full investigation of the plant. These guys are not going to get away, but we want to make sure they don't injure or kill their hostage. In the meantime, we're on the way."

"We?" came the confused voice of Winkowski.

"Yeah, me . . ." and she paused, "and my secret weapon.."

19

ROMMEL HAD THE sense of him.

It had returned, going off in the back of his head like a light bulb. Suddenly, just like that, Rommel was *aware* of Chuck, that dim background sensation that was part of the link they shared. He still couldn't communicate with Chuck. Chances were Chuck wasn't even aware that the link had been reestablished. Maybe he hadn't even realized that it had been severed. Humans could be pretty thick that way.

He started moving through the forest, having left the cabin with Dakota far behind him. There was nothing he could do for her anyway, and even if there was, he didn't have much interest in it. For whatever reason, Chuck was keeping her around, but Rommel had little to no patience with her.

He hated to admit it, but Rommel was also fairly tired. He hadn't eaten in ages, hadn't slept. He was getting exhausted.

Something small darted just within his field of vision and he started after it, hoping against hope that it was something he could eat. A flash of white, a small tail, told him it was a rabbit. Well, maybe the spirit of Chuck had somehow invaded his mind and, annoyingly, distorted his sense of priorities, but nothing was going to stop him from chowing down on a rabbit.

He bore down on the rabbit, barking eagerly, knowing that

giving the animal warning was not the brightest maneuver, but unable to contain his enthusiasm.

The rabbit spun and snarled at him.

That brought Rommel up short. The rabbit glared at him through red eyes and bared its teeth. It was the largest damned rabbit Rommel had ever seen.

It was *growling*. Madness. He'd never heard a rabbit make the slightest noise at all, and this one sounded like it was about to leap for the kill.

Which was exactly what it did. Two, three hops and the rabbit was slicing though the air at Rommel, ready to fight, ready to kill.

Rommel crushed its skull with one swipe of his paw.

He looked down disdainfully at the corpse in front of him. Killer or no, it was still just a rabbit, for pity's sake. Nothing that Rommel couldn't handle.

He tore off a piece of the rabbit's carcass with his teeth and chomped on it, and then he promptly spit it out. He knew immediately that something was wrong, that there was some sort of deadly additional ingredient to the rabbit's makeup. It was not something he wanted to have anything to do with, but unfortunately, that meant that he was going to have to continue being hungry. There was, he realized, no help for that.

He kept walking, trying to get a feel for what direction Chuck was in. It was possible Chuck might simply find his way to Rommel, but he decided he wasn't going to just stand around and wait. Chuck was a nice enough guy for a human, Rommel decided, but not exactly big on brain power. He couldn't always be counted on to do the simple, intelligent thing. Rommel had lost count of the number of times he had had to do the thinking for both of them. Making up for humanity's shortcomings was one of the many burdens that animals had to uphold.

He'd heard Chuck use the phrase "beasts of burden." Maybe that was what it referred to.

Rommel scoured the area, trying to track Chuck, and eventually settled on one particular direction as being the most promising. There was no one reason he could pin down as to why he felt that way. Just a general impression. He hoped it was the right one.

In the cabin that Rommel had left behind, Mars placed his muzzle down on his front paws. Mars had sensed another dog in the area, but now that dog had moved on. It was obviously not going to challenge Mars's claim on the area. Too bad, Mars decided. Some large animal to rip apart would have gone down quite nicely about now.

Dakota, from the corner, her knees pulled up, watched Mars carefully and said, 'Your dog seems kind of fidgety. Maybe he has to go out.''

''Maybe he does,'' agreed Jupiter. ''But we're all holding it. So can he.''

''You're all heart.''

She turned back and looked at Shai. The large, dark man had been staring at her for some time now, just staring at her. It was starting to get on her nerves. ''And what do you want?'' she asked with some impatience.

He grinned at her disarmingly. He seemed so pleasant, even amused by it all. There was a detachment about him, as if he considered everything that occurred as merely of a transitory nature.

''What's your name?'' he asked her. ''And come on . . . let's can the bullshit, okay?'' He had that curious, hinting bit of an accent. The question came out ''cahn the bullsheet.''

And suddenly it really did seem somewhat ridiculous. ''Dakota,'' she said.

''Right, first name North,'' said Jupiter, the gaze of his narrow eyes darting from one to the other.

''No, that's her name,'' said Shai with confidence. ''At least the name she goes by on a regular basis. First name or last?''

"Both. Originally first, but I dropped the last one ages ago." Dakota was becomingly increasingly convinced that she was never going to make it out of here. There was a kind of bleak certainty that this was it, and that being the case, what was the point in jerking around anymore. "I thought it would look better to have just the one name. More mysterious." She put up a hand as if envisioning the name stretched across a marquee. "Da-Ko-Ta," she said, adding a breathless pause to each syllable.

"Very mysterious," agreed Shai. He shook his head. "Silly lady. You're no more with the Complex than I am."

"I dunno, you with the Complex?" She smiled.

"If I were, Da-Ko-Ta, I wouldn't be here."

"Go ahead, tell him the truth," said Jupiter with an expansive wave. "Tell him whatever you want, because I already know the truth and nothing you can say is going to convince me otherwise."

She shook her head, a neutral expression on her face. "It must be wonderful to be that smart, that you can't ever be fooled."

"It carries a certain degree of responsibility," he conceded. "I try to live up to it."

Dakota brought her hands above her head, interlacing her fingers, and cracked her knuckles loudly. She glanced over at Luta and, to her surprise, saw that the smaller woman had curled up in a corner and gone to sleep. Well, that was certainly one way to escape from pressure.

"So what are you doing here?" asked Shai.

She smiled thinly. Screw it. "I don't know," she said. "There was this guy . . . and he seemed really nice. Was really nice. He showed up in the circus I was working at—I was a tightrope walker. And he stayed with us for a while, but then guys who were after him showed up and he wasn't going to be able to stay anymore. And the circus life had really started to drag for me."

"How did you come to join the circus?"

She stared at him. "You got a smoke?"

"Buzz smoked. He was killed and tossed out a window."

"That's one way to kick the habit," she acknowledged.

Shai grinned widely at that and inclined his head at Luta. "Good thing she's asleep. She'd start blubbering, she hear you say that."

"She liked Buzz?"

"She likes living. Buzz didn't live, that shook her up."

Jupiter cleared his throat loudly. "I hope you two are having a nice chat," he said somewhat petulantly.

Shai's smile seemed to say, *Ignore him.* "So, why the circus?" he repeated.

She shrugged. "Usual reason. Ran away when I was a teenager. Circus was a haven. Didn't run away from much. Father who was a drunk and lorded it over all of us." She paused. "My mother never stood up to him. I always hated her for that. Why she put up with it I'll never know."

"So you've never been home in all that time."

She paused. "Got word two months ago, my no-good father hit the road."

"You mean he left?"

"No, he hit the road. He staggered drunk one night into the middle of the interstate and a cross-country truck banged into him." She smacked a fist into her palm. "Sent him flying about, oh, twenty, thirty yards. They collected the remains with a teaspoon."

He was silent for a moment. "I'm sorry."

"Yeah, well, that makes one of us. And my mother wanted me to come home. Apologized for everything, apologized for being weak and not standing up to him."

"And did you? Go home, I mean?"

She looked at him. "No."

"Why not?"

"Why should I?"

"Because she asked you to. Because if I were your parent

and I had not done right by you, I'd want the chance to make amends.''

"Yeah, well . . . we don't always get what we want." She paused, and sighed. "But after that, the circus seemed . . . I dunno, I guess after ten years of going everywhere, you suddenly start feeling like you're going nowhere. Y'know? So when Chuck came along . . ."

"Chuck was the bearded fellow," said Jupiter.

"Yeah."

"The fellow Shai shot and killed. On my orders."

She stared at Shai, her eyes narrowing. He said nothing, and at last she said, "No he didn't."

"Ah, well, obviously a decade of circus life has made you wise in all things," Jupiter said.

"Wiser than you, smartass," said Dakota. She shook her head. "I'd kill for a cigarette."

"Tell you what," said Jupiter. "We'll see if we can scrape one up for you . . . at the time of your execution. Think of it as a last request."

"I'll always remember your compassion," said Dakota dryly. She glanced at Shai and, with a toss of her head in Jupiter's direction, said, "Why hang out with this idiot?"

Jupiter made a bemused *humph* sound. Shai raised an eloquent eyebrow. "I promised I would."

"Promised him?"

"Promised my family," he said. "On their graves. Promised I would do something, try to help others to avoid the fate they had. Don't know how much I've succeeded. You try, and you do what you can. But there's this overwhelming sense of—I don't know—hopelessness. Because every day we wake up, on the run, looking over our shoulders because we're certain that someone is going to catch up with us and kill us just about anytime. And what are we fighting for? The gray skies that are overhead. Still gray. Just as gray as when I started this fight ages ago. Maybe even grayer. And you got to wonder, what is the point of it all? What's the damned point?''

She shrugged. ''Beats me. I'm just a dumb circus performer.''

''Yes, that is what you would have us believe,'' said Jupiter sarcastically. ''But that's a useless ploy.''

''Well, I just don't have a hope in hell of slipping one past you, do I?'' Dakota asked him.

He shook his head. ''I've seen too many lies. I'm too good at spotting them.''

''No, you just assume that everything is a lie. It's not the same thing.''

''Nowadays, my dear Screw, it's generally a safe assumption. A very, very safe assumption.''

She stared at Jupiter for a time. ''We're not going to get out of here, are we?''

''Is this some sort of revelation that just hit you?''

''Kind of.''

''Well, my dear, that is the project that I'm working on. To live or not live, survive or not survive. And a great deal of that hinges on the desirability of a certain Complex agent. That, my dear, had better be you.''

''Up close and personal, Jupiter. One on one, you and me, no more bullshit, I'm telling you—I'm not who you think I am.''

He smiled at that. ''Which of us is, my dear Screw? Which of us is?''

20

JO WAS BEGINNING to wonder if she hadn't made a mistake.

The path they were following up the mountainside had widened out, and Chuck had asked her indulgence while he stopped briefly to rest. Now he was sitting on a flat rock, cross-legged, breathing slowly, sightless eyes staring at nothing, and he had been that way for several minutes.

"Would you mind telling me what in hell you think you're doing?" she asked, her impatience mounting.

"You're standing"—he paused—"six feet away."

She looked down, mentally measuring the expanse of ground between them. "About, yeah."

"And you're . . . there," and he pointed straight at her. "So?"

"I need you to do something for me."

"If it will get us moving." She glanced over her shoulder and saw the sun beginning to come up on the horizon. Thank God. It had been the longest night of her life. It also brought them closer, though, to the deadline of 0900. Didn't he understand that? Didn't he care?

"I need you to move. As quietly as you can. And if you can, try and get close enough to touch me without my knowing."

He was pointing at her, and every instinct about him seemed to be directed at her.

Okay then. If that was what he wanted to play. She began to move as silently as she could, knees flexed, one foot quietly crossing in front of the other, hands out to the side for balance.

His pointing hand slowly followed her, tracking her. She raised an eyebrow and had to admit to herself that she was impressed. Then she abruptly switched direction, arcing back the way that she had come.

He continued to point where she had been, and she felt slightly disappointed in him. Then his finger wavered, and he was clearly confused. He didn't know where she was, but he knew that she wasn't where she had been.

She picked up a rock that was lying nearby and tossed it to her left. The clattering on the ground distracted him and he looked off in the direction of the rock. As he did so, she came in quickly, her hand streaking out.

Her hand clamped down tightly on his shoulder and she dug her fingernails in. "Ow!" he said. "Come on, that hurt."

"Would have hurt a lot more if I had a knife in my hand. What are you trying to prove?"

"I'm not trying to prove anything. I'm trying to learn." He frowned. "Trying to remember things my sensei taught me. Things he said that maybe I didn't even fully understand when he was teaching me. I should be able to keep track of you."

"You're blind, Chuck," she said harshly. "I really don't mean to upset you or anything, but it's pretty obvious."

"I should be part of nature," he said stubbornly. "As you are. If we're part of the same world, I should be able to know where you are. I should be able to feel you at all times."

"Not on a first date. Now come on." She started to walk away.

"No."

She made an angry, guttural sound in her throat, stomped back and stood in front of him. "You are so goddamn stubborn it's not funny. I'm ordering you to come on."

"I'm fighting for my life here!" he said angrily. "Don't you understand that?"

"What I understand is that I've been given a deadline by a bunch of terrorist loons, and your own partner has her life on the line, and you're sitting here giving me bullshit about being part of nature. Have you seen nature lately, pal? Believe me, it's not something you'd want to be a part of. Now move it."

"Leave me if you have to. But I won't be any good to Dakota—to anyone—unless I learn to handle this. I can't be afraid of the dark. It has to make no difference."

"Christ!" she said angrily, and she reached for him.

Chuck wasn't even thinking about it, didn't even realize her hand was outstretched. But his right arm swung up automatically and brushed it aside.

They stood there that way for a moment, unmoving. Then slowly Jo backed up a couple of steps, pondering the situation.

She tried to grab him again. He blocked it.

A slow smile was beginning to spread across his face.

Both of her hands moved incredibly quickly now, trying to grab hold of him, trying to fake him out. He didn't go for the fakes, wasn't fooled by them at all, and the other, closer strikes he swept aside. They moved so quickly, parry and thrust, that it was a blur.

He managed to block ten of her thrusts. On the eleventh her left hand sailed through while he was blocking her right and she slapped him hard across the face. The loud *crack* seemed to jostle him for a moment, and then he rubbed his face and half smiled. "Not bad. Not a bad start."

"Yeah, well, it's going to have to do. Now come on."

He nodded briskly, sliding off the rock. He still wasn't fully confident, still had a way to go, but he was starting to feel a little better.

He stepped forward and tripped over a gopher hole.

Jo turned to see him sprawled out on the ground. "Every

couple of steps forward you wind up taking a few back, don't you, cowboy?''

"Sure looks that way, doesn't it?''

Slowly he climbed to his feet, shaking his head. Then he looked up at her, and he frowned. "My God,'' he said.

"What is it?''

"I'm starting to see something. Vague . . . very vague shadows at best. More confusing than anything else at the moment, but I think . . . yeah.'' His voice started to become more excited. "Hold up some fingers.''

She held up two fingers.

"Five,'' he said. "Am I right? Five?''

"Well, five if you count the three that were clenched, yeah. Come on.''

Feeling somewhat crestfallen but nevertheless a bit better, Chuck followed her up the narrow trail.

And then, ahead of them, they heard screams. And a very familiar roar.

And something else. Something that galvanized Chuck into action, and with a shout he shoved past Jo and started running and stumbling in the direction of the furious animal sounds. Jo couldn't believe it. Whatever was going on up ahead was clearly something involving some very angry and very nasty-sounding animals—possibly more of those mutant bears that she had dealt with. It was not an encounter she was looking forward to and yet, thanks to the blind superman, she had to go running straight into the maw of the danger again.

Oh, hell, she reasoned. No one said she was going to live forever. And she ran after Chuck up the path.

21

THE CUTTERS WERE relatively new to the woods. They had found that abandoned cabin, the one that they'd now been forced to give up. The nice thing about it was that it had been built so close to the edge of a passage that led up the cliffside. It made it easily accessible to the main road. They followed that passage up now, cursing and muttering to themselves over the unfairness of all that had gone on.

"Our cabin."

"Damned right."

"Our bedrolls."

"Damned right."

"She had no damned right!"

"Damned right."

And so on, as they trudged up the passage and eventually up into the woods that lay at the top.

In their anger and loud cursings, they aroused the mutant bear that had been sleeping in the brush just near the top of the passage, the part that opened out onto a clearing at the top. The bear had lost a lot of blood—the many bullet wounds it had received had weakened it. But there was still a lot of life left in the old creature, and it had no intention of expiring quietly. But it was indeed much too slow to wake up in time to do little more than grunt at the men who went by. And that they did not even hear.

So they went past, and eventually the bear staggered to its feet and headed off in a particular direction.

The Cutters, meantime, made their way through the woods, and then the foremost jumped back and uttered a shriek.

"What is it?" demanded the other, already more than fed up with the miserable way matters had turned out.

"Look!" said the first Cutter urgently, and the one bringing up the rear looked where he was pointing.

They saw bodies of soldiers lying there, unmoving, and the soft sound of flies. The men moved forward cautiously, brushing away the pesky insects that were swarming around the dead soldiers. They looked as if they'd been gutted from crotch to sternum.

All of which was of little interest to the two Cutters. What caught their fancy far more, and what pleased them no end, was that the bodies had guns on them. Guns in their hands or guns in their holsters.

"Let's get 'em," said the taller of the two, and his compatriot did not hesitate. There were three soldiers there, and within moments, the two Cutters had divested them of their weaponry.

The taller Cutter was joyfully buckling the ammo belt on. The shorter was sighting through a special scope, and he saw that a pin-width beam of red laser light emitted from the scope, drawing a bead on whatever it was aimed at. That way you knew, every time.

"Damn, this thing is great," he said. He swept it around and the red light played ominously on the forehead of his friend who made it clear in turn that he was not thrilled one bit. "I know you've been saying we shouldn't hang out too long in the woods, because of some of the things wandering around here. But this baby'll—"

"You jackass, get that thing off me!" he snarled. "Find something else to aim at—"

They suddenly became immobile as they heard the sound

of something making its way through the woods. Not an inch did they move.

Rommel made his way through the forest, proceeding as cautiously as he could. He was operating entirely on instinct, which was not unusual for him. But this time it was to an extraordinary degree. He had not picked up any sort of scent of Chuck. He had no proof from any of his other senses that Chuck was ahead of him, or that he was heading in the right direction. Nothing except a deep and abiding faith in the infallibility of his basic nature.

In other words, he was too self-confident to think that he could possibly be wrong.

The wind was to Rommel's back and then it shifted. That shift brought Rommel up short, because a new and somewhat odious scent reached his nostrils. He paused, his ears pricked high, his eyes narrowing ferally. The scent . . . was familiar. Human, yes, Rommel had known that immediately. But also human—no, humans—that he had encountered before. Yes, that was it. It was some of those humans whom they had encountered earlier, outside the eating place.

Did they have Chuck? It was a wondrous burst of intuitive possibility on Rommel's part. He knew that they had menaced Chuck earlier, if the threat that such as they provided could actually be termed ''menace.'' If they had Chuck, they'd probably hurt him if they could . . . *if* they could. Maybe he was even with them. It seemed very unlikely to Rommel—he would certainly smell Chuck, or sense him through their link.

And then Rommel hit on . . . a plan.

Now German shepherds—even telepathic ones that were built like small cars—were not known for their extensive strategic capabilities. Rommel had even once had a lengthy argument with Chuck over that very subject, when they had been having one of their customary discussions over the infinite superiority of man's best friend over man. This was not, curiously, a view to which Chuck subscribed, and Rommel could not understand why. Chuck had contended that man's ability to plan strategy made him somehow better than dogs. His proof had been to point to the roster of famous military strategists throughout the history of mankind. Rommel's response had been that if that was Chuck's proof of superiority, it was pretty pathetic because (as Rommel sanguinely pointed out) you never saw dogs being stupid enough to get into organized wars in the first place.

Chuck's explanation of reasons for war wasn't much better. Primarily, it seemed, humans fought over imaginary lines called *boundaries*. Rommel couldn't grasp fighting over something that wasn't there. The least humans could have the courtesy of doing, Rommel felt, was urinating on what was theirs so everyone would know whose was what. That would probably eliminate wars. Chuck tended to agree, feeling that if it had been pissed on, nobody else would want it anyway.

The upshot of the ongoing discussions was that the subtleties of human behavior continued to elude Rommel, or had until just now when he came up with . . . *a plan*.

It was not a deep plan, or a subtle plan. But it was a plan nevertheless, and Rommel felt some measure of pride in it.

What he planned was quite simple, really. He would wait until the foolish humans showed themselves. Then he would bare his teeth and bark very viciously. The humans would run screaming to a place of safety, and that place of safety might be, hopefully *would* be, where they were keeping Chuck. And if he found Chuck, then hopefully Chuck would feed him since, thus far, nothing he'd encountered in the woods had been vaguely appetizing.

If Chuck was not there, Rommel had even developed (wonder of wonders) a *backup plan*. Namely that he'd kill the humans and eat them, and mental directives and taboos and queasy feelings be damned, he was hungry for pity's sake and if his next meal had to be human flesh, and he had to eventually face Chuck and be scolded for it, so be it. At least he'd be scolded on a full stomach.

Rommel waited for them, quiet and still, in a small clearing. They sounded like bulldozers coming through the woods, and Rommel realized that they were actually under the impression that they were being sneaky. Infinitely superior humans indeed. It was to laugh, ha ha.

The humans burst into the clearing and skidded to a halt. If Rommel had had the facial muscles to smile, he would have. The look on their faces was absolutely priceless.

They recognized him, of that Rommel was certain. He growled for effect, and then barked loudly to get them running.

They didn't run. Instead they swung around human guns and aimed them right at Rommel.

Rommel's heart sank. This was definitely not good.

The first bullet kicked up dirt just in front of him. Rommel leaped back with a yelp, and the second bullet blew out a branch just to Rommel's left.

Rommel came to the sudden realization that his plan was shot, and he might be next. His backup plan seemed even more remote than the primary plan.

With an alarmed bark, he pivoted and leaped into the woods. There was another gunshot and he felt a brief flash of pain on his left flank. A bullet had just winged him, and he had absolutely no intention of hanging around in case one of the bullets should strike closer.

He bolted through the woods, bullets flying all around him. Yes, this was most definitely not good.

It had been a good plan, a noble plan. It just happened not to have worked.

The Cutters laughed uproariously and they fired again on the fleeing form of the dog. It was so big that it couldn't slink away as a smaller animal might. Instead, it left brush waving in its wake.

The Cutters looked at each other, and didn't even have to tell each other what was on their respective minds. They both plunged into the woods after the dog, the sound of it just ahead of them pulling them on.

Rommel heard them coming after him and his heart sank even further. Whenever he slowed down in the slightest, there would be the sounds of gunfire and brush would be broken off around him. He wasn't sure if they were toying with him, or if they were just miserable shots.

The bushes pulled and yanked at his fur, and the ground began to tear at the pads of his paws. He was tired—dog-tired. He had had no sleep, no food. Nothing. Even at his peak, he probably couldn't jump them fast enough to take them out before one of them managed to drill him. As it was the wound on his flank was stabbing at him, slowing him down.

There was the constant sound of joyous whoops and hollerings. God, it was annoying. It was hard enough for Rommel to think, since thinking had never been his specialty. It was not being made any easier by the constant chattering and bellowing of those idiots behind him.

Then he picked up another scent.

It slowed him down momentarily, and a bullet missed him by scant inches (the morons were definitely catching up), but he had to home in on the direction. *There!* There it most definitely was, and he headed off, tracing the scent, his heart pounding with excitement.

He had come up with *another plan*! Three plans in the course of fifteen minutes, a record not only for him, but possibly for all dogs everywhere.

For a moment the Cutters thought they had lost track of him. Then they heard a rustling off to their right and barreled off in that direction.

Their enthusiasm was at an all-time high. They were envisioning doggie insides splattered all over the landscape, bits of fur sticking to the sides of the trees that towered all around them. It was a pleasant and diverting thought, and their only concern was that they might lose the beast and so be deprived of not only their pleasure but a nice bit of revenge. For they had not forgotten that this was the animal that had nearly killed their friend, their leader, their constant and bosom companion, good ol' what's-his-name.

They broke from cover, looking around, and the taller one pointed. Sure enough, there was the stupid dog, pausing at the top of what seemed to be a path that angled downward. If the dog had made a break straight down without stopping, it might actually have gotten away. But it was sitting there, as if waiting for them. Stupid dog.

"Niiiiice doggie," said the shorter one, and the red light of the laser sight appeared on Rommel's forehead. A split instant later the gun fired, but Rommel was no longer there. Instead he had run off down the angled path.

"Forget it, he's gone," said the taller.

"No! Come on! He's gonna pay."

"We're wasting our ammo. He's just a dumb mutt."

"I don't like the way he looked at me. Like he thinks I'm a jerk or something." And with that he ran down the path after his quarry.

His companion stood there for a moment, shaking his head. "You are a jerk!" he called after him, and then with a sigh slammed in another clip and went off after his buddy. With his longer strides he caught up within moments.

They noticed that the barking up ahead had stopped, that the dog must be moving stealthily now. But the path was narrow, the sides sheer as it wended down the cliffside. They were unsure whether it was a natural formation or man-made, and ultimately it didn't matter. All that mattered was that they were going to nail themselves a canine would-be murderer. And there was nowhere, absolutely nowhere, that the stupid animal was going to be able to hide.

They turned a blind corner and skidded to a halt, their laughter and amusement catching in their throats.

Blocking their path was a huge bear. Not just any bear—this thing was beyond all belief. It was unnatural. Its dark fur was covered with dried blood from multiple wounds inflicted on its body. Wounds created by guns such as the Cutters were carrying. The bear wasn't moving, instead was lying on its side, its eyes closed.

Dropping his voice to barely a whisper, the taller one said, "It's dead. Right?"

Abruptly, with a sound like a furnace, the bear's chest rose and fell.

"It's sleeping," said the shorter one, equally as quietly. "And it's got bullet holes all over it. And that didn't kill it."

"Let's get the hell out of here," said the taller.

And at that moment, from directly behind the sleeping animal, Rommel poked his head up. The men looked at him in confusion, and then the great German shepherd drew his head back and clamped his jaws down with all his strength on the bear's hindquarters.

The great animal rose up with a roar, awakened rudely from its sleep. The ground seemed to rumble in harmony with the fury of the bear. And in its towering rage, the very first thing it saw was the Cutters.

Upon seeing the attack and the sheer power of the angry beast, the taller of the two men became rooted to the spot, whimpering and blubbering. The shorter started to run and got a couple of yards when he heard a hideous scream, the sound of rending flesh, and he turned in time to see his partner's entrails spilling down the path. The dog was watching with great interest.

The bear turned its malevolent gaze on the Cutter, a gaze that seemed to say, *You did this to me. You and your kind.* It took one stalking step toward him.

The Cutter brought his beloved gun up. The red light shone square between the bear's eyes and he fired twice, three times.

It drilled the monster, blowing off the top of its skull and splattering its brains onto the tree next to it. One eye was gone, the other unseeing.

Barely able to believe his triumph, the Cutter let out a joyful laugh as the bear fell—

—on top of the Cutter. He was flattened under it, the bear's massive tonnage crushing him instantly, the laughter dying along with the rest of him.

Rommel stared at the mess, shaking his great head slowly. What in the world made humans think that they had the slightest prayer when it came to matching wits with dogs?

Then a familiar presence made itself known in his mind. He turned excitedly, calling out, *Chuck?*

Chuck came running up the path and cried out in delight. He charged toward Rommel and tripped on some brush. He fell, absorbing the impact, but Rommel was instantly alerted.

You can't see, he said in shock.

"I can't see, right," said Chuck. "Well, a little bit—vague shadows, distinguishing between light and dark. How are you?"

Hungry.

"Nice to know there are some things you can count on."

Suddenly Rommel lifted his head, growling low in his throat. Immediately Chuck knew what he was reacting to and said, as softly as he could, "She's a friend. She doesn't know about us. Be subtle."

Behind Chuck now came Jo, looking puzzled and shaking her head. "Chuck, who is . . ." Then she gasped, upon seeing the carnage. "My God," she breathed.

"What is it?" he said urgently. "What's wrong?"

"I—I was going to ask you who the dog is . . . but that can wait. Just ahead of us . . . there's a dead bear, and two dead men."

"Your men?"

"Civilians."

"I wonder who they are," said Chuck, but the tone was significant enough that Rommel knew to whom the question was addressed.

Two of the idiots who were bothering you back at the eating place.

"Cutters," said Chuck, understanding.

"Could be," agreed Jo. "Wait—yeah, that's them, all right. They're kind of bloody and messed up, so I didn't recognize them right off, but they were the ones who were hassling you back at the cabin."

"Even so, they didn't deserve to die," said Chuck.

"Well, they sure weren't earning the Congressional Medal while they were living. So who, or what, is this magnificent animal?"

"Rommel. He's my dog."

"Looks more like your dogs, plural. Okay, come on, let's get to Winkowski. He must be going nuts up there."

"Right. You lead the way."

Jo nodded, gingerly stepping over the remains of the bear and the men. She extended a hand to Chuck who climbed over the obstruction, and then headed up the path. Behind her Chuck slowed down long enough to say softly to Rommel, "Any idea what those men were doing here?"

Dying, mostly, said Rommel after a moment of thought.

22

THE SOUND OF the chopper roused them.

Jupiter, without thinking, ran to the window of the cabin and glanced out. At the last minute he checked his forward motion, narrowly avoiding providing a target for whatever snipers might be out there. Still, in the dimness of the dark dawn, he was able to make out an army helicopter whipping past them high overhead.

"Our ride is here," he said tightly.

It roused Luta from her slumber. Shai, for his part, made no movement, but said simply, "They'll never let us go, Jupe. Got no reason."

"We have a reason," said Jupiter tightly, pointing at Dakota. "She's our reason."

"She's a little girl from the circus," Shai replied. "You don't want to admit we're dead, but we are. But you keep clinging onto this hope that she's our ticket out. She's not."

Slowly Jupiter approached Shai, as if he were trying to stare him down. "She will be," he said tightly, "what I want her to be."

"Shai, what if he's right," said Luta slowly.

"He's not right."

"I'll prove it," said Jupiter, and suddenly there was a gun in his hand. A small dainty pistol, and he held it to Dakota's head. Shai's eyes glowered in the dark, and Jupiter told her, "Tell him you're with the Complex."

Dakota's gaze slowly went from Jupiter to Shai and back again. She knew what the score was. She saw the wildness in Jupiter's eyes. Penned up here, not knowing what was outside, knowing in his heart that the end was near but not able to admit it, Jupiter was starting to crack. Perhaps he had already cracked. There was intense desperation in his eyes, the kind of raw, throbbing emotion that couldn't be reckoned with, couldn't be bargained with, but could only be feared.

"I'm with the Complex," she said.

Jupiter stayed like that for a time longer. "I knew it. See? I told you." He slowly drew back the gun, a glimmer of triumph filling his eyes.

"Sure. You told me," said Shai. "Old, stupid me."

Jupiter's gaze suddenly darted quickly, nervously. "Where'd the helicopter go?" he said.

"Gone, man," said Shai, shaking his head. "Wasn't for us. Army's bringing more guys is what. Then they're going to rush the place, and they're not going to care about some little circus girl getting filled with holes."

"Shut up." The command was low and fierce, and then repeated with clear, careful articulation. "Shut the hell up," and Jupiter was pointing the gun at Shai.

The two men glowered at each other, and Luta looked fearfully at Jupiter. "Put it down, Jupiter," she said.

"No."

"Put it down or I'll make it stop working."

He looked at her, impressed. "You'd do that?"

"Yes, to protect Shai." There was surprising strength in her voice, as if the pressure had galvanized her. Backed against the wall, she had come to realize that there was nothing more for her to lose. "To protect all of us. I'm—I'm scared, Jupiter. I still am. But I'm even more scared for you than I am for myself. I don't want you to be hurt, or for you to hurt Shai. So, yes, I would short-circuit your gun."

He actually looked hurt. It was the first time that Dakota had seen any real emotion play across his face. He had kept himself wrapped so tightly, but the cracks were there. They had always been there. They were just harder to see.

"I thought you loved me," and there was betrayal in his voice.

"I do," she said softly. "But I'll stop you if I have to."

He regarded her for a time longer. "You know . . . I think you would."

And he shot her.

Dakota jumped and shrieked as Luta pitched back. She slammed her head against the wall of the cabin and slumped down, leaving a trail of blood marking her slide like a ghoulish road map. Mars barked furiously at the sudden noise, confused and upset.

Jupiter's mask of impassiveness had been replaced. He glanced back at Shai, who made no move, no sound. "Anything to say?" Jupiter asked him.

Shai shrugged. "Never liked her anyway."

Dakota looked at him, appalled. Did he mean it? Did he say it just to accommodate what was clearly a crazy man in the cabin with them? She couldn't tell. His face was unreadable.

Jupiter raised his voice, shouting as loudly as he could, so that his voice would carry. "That could have been your agent," he called. "She might be dead right now! You'd better bring that helicopter back again!"

Dakota started to move toward Luta and Jupiter said sharply, "You'd better stay where you are."

She looked back at him, fixed him with a stare that sparked with all the fury, all the anger and tired rage that she had left in her. Once she had been concerned about being shot. Once, in what seemed ages ago. Now she was cold and tired and hungry. Her hair hung in limp, lifeless strands. Every muscle ached, every bone creaked, and she simply didn't care anymore.

"If you're going to pull the trigger," she said in a hoarse whisper, "pull it and be damned. Otherwise shut the fuck up."

She went to Luta and braced herself, waiting for the smack of a bullet between her shoulder blades. But none was forthcoming. She checked the woman over, found profuse bleeding from her shoulder and her face dead white. She was clearly going into shock. Dakota tore off a piece of her shirt and tried to stanch the bleeding as best she could, and desperately tried to remember what you do for something like this. Elevate the head or the feet, one or the other. She wasn't sure which. But from the way the girl was bleeding, it wasn't going to matter pretty soon.

"Bring us the helicopter," Jupiter shouted again, "or she dies!"

And then a voice called out, strong and loud, and there were reactions of astonishment from everyone within the cabin.

"I have some unfinished business with one of your men," the voice called, "and if he's not a coward . . . he'll come out here and finish it!"

23

Jo's VOICE CRACKLED over Winkowski's comm unit. He grabbed at it with relief as she said, "Pigeon Six, you there?"

"Right here, Panther Six," he sighed. He was a nervous wreck, his concentration shot from having to monitor hour after hour the lack of movement outside the cabin. "Where are you?"

"Right behind you," came the reply.

He turned slowly and saw Jo's face smiling lopsidedly behind him. "Nice to know you're on top of things, Pigeon Six."

He sagged. "Boy, am I glad to see you." Then his eyes narrowed. "Who's that?"

"Oh, him," and she inclined her head toward Chuck, who had appeared from the undergrowth next to her. "That there is Chuck. He's a new recruit."

"Hi there," and he extended a hand, and then yanked it back in alarm, bringing his gun up in the same motion. *"What the hell—!"*

"Oh, that's Rommel," she added dryly. Next to Chuck, Rommel had appeared, teeth bared. He was still not especially pleased by the proximity of soldiers, and least of all their weapons.

At that moment her comm unit crackled to life. She and

Winkowski looked at each other in surprise and she plucked it off her belt. "Panther Six here."

A brusque male voice said, "Panther One-one here."

Major Sutphin. "Well, it's about goddamn time!" she said in exasperation. "Where the hell have you been?!"

"Panther Six, I can't say I appreciate your tone."

She was about to tell him where he could shove his appreciation, but she glanced at Winkowski crouched next to her, hanging on her every word. "Sorry, sir," she said, trying her best to sound contrite. "It's been . . . a difficult night." (Good God, had it all been in one night?)

"Understood," was the terse reply. "We are approaching via helicarrier."

"May I respectfully ask the major," she said, "where you've been all this time?"

"Inspecting the damage at Internet Propulsion and combing the surrounding area."

"But I dispatched three men to Internet! They should have told you that we had the Extremists pinned down!"

"Yes, well . . . unfortunately, your men were shot."

Jo's jaw dropped and she and Winkowski exchanged incredulous looks. *"Shot?"*

"That's affirmative."

"By *who*?"

"The guard at the factory. He mistook them for intruders and shot them as they forced their way though the front gate. One is dead, the other two are in a coma."

Jo looked at Winkowski, and then at Chuck. Chuck, sensing her eyes on him, said, as if by way of explanation, "The guard was confused when I saw him."

"You saw him. Before he shot my men."

"That's right."

"And you didn't kill him."

"There seemed little reason to at the time," he said dryly. Suddenly a helicopter hurtled toward them, and as it did so the major's voice crackled over the comm unit, "Give us your position, Panther Six."

"You'll be directly over our position on my mark . . . now!" said Jo as the chopper flew directly overhead. Then she added, "You saw the cabin?"

"That's affirmative. That where the Extremists are holed up?"

"Yes, sir."

"Excellent. We'll be there with reinforcements momentarily. Hold on. Panther One-one out."

The comm unit clicked off, and that's when they heard the gunshot.

"Oh, my God," whispered Chuck, "Dakota . . ."

He started to stand up and Jo yanked him down roughly. "What're you, nuts?" she snapped. "Don't present a target like that. Don't give them any hint as to your location. That's why I had Winkowski maintaining radio silence, so his yap wouldn't give his position away. Although if I'd known my three men were shot before they could pass information along . . ." And she shook her head. "Twenty-twenty hindsight."

Then they heard a voice, the angry voice shouting, "That could have been your agent! She might be dead right now! You'd better bring that helicopter back again!"

"That's one of the men from the factory, all right," said Chuck confidently. "I'd know that voice anywhere."

"We have to stall them until the reinforcements show up," said Winkowski. "Their deadline was oh-nine-hundred hours. We have time yet."

"That was not the voice of a man who's got all his soldiers in a row," said Jo. "He's cracking. I can hear it. And when he goes off, his gun will go off. We've got to do something to keep him occupied."

"I'll do it," said Chuck.

She looked at him incredulously, as did Winkowski. "You've gotta be shitting me," she told him.

"That's army talk, right?"

"Those creeps are responsible for at least a dozen deaths," Jo said. "I'm not going to put another one into their laps."

"Neither am I," Chuck told her. "Especially when that other woman is a woman who's a friend of mine. Now I'm doing this. I'm expendable. Besides . . . I owe them."

"You owe them?" Her tone was dangerous.

"One of them, at any rate. He could've killed me. He didn't. He's entitled to another shot at me, the way he wants it. I always pay my debts."

"Even if you pay with your life."

He nodded slowly. "Even if."

Chuck stepped away from her and moved into the brush, Rommel following. Jo made no move to stop him, and Winkowski said in surprise, "You're just letting him go?"

"I think I have to," she said.

Chuck made his way through the brush, Rommel at his side. He kept one hand resting lightly on Rommel's back as the dog guided him toward the cabin. "You're going to be my eyes, Rommel."

I was getting that impression.

"This is going to be very important. I'm counting on you, because that guy can kill me, even hand-to-hand. I'm certain of it."

That would make life fairly dull, if you weren't around.

He almost laughed at that. "I'd miss you, too."

I didn't say I'd miss you. I could use a little boredom.

He went a few feet farther and then stopped. "There's an open space in front of us, isn't there?"

Yes.

"Describe it to me."

What do you want to know?

"Whatever's important."

Okay. There's no food there.

Chuck sighed. "Is there anything that's an obstruction on it?"

No, it's fairly flat.

"Where's the cabin?"

Over on the other side of the clearing.

"How far?"

What?

"How far? How many yards or meters?"

I give up. How many?

Chuck realized he had a problem. "Okay, look . . . if you had a whole bunch of dogs your size lying end to end, from here to there, how many dogs would it take to reach the cabin?"

There was a dead silence.

What in hell are you talking about?

"Dumb dog."

Get neutered.

Chuck sighed, more deeply this time. All right then, the hard way. He cupped his hands to his mouth and shouted, "I have some unfinished business with one of your men, and if he's not a coward . . . he'll come out here and finish it!"

24

DAKOTA STILL COULDN'T believe it. Chuck! Alive! She wanted to call him, to shout out that she was okay, that everything was going to be okay.

Jupiter and Shai stared at each other. "Did my ears deceive me," said Jupiter slowly, "or did I just hear the voice of a dead man call out to me?"

"I guess I missed," said Shai.

"I wanted him dead."

"You'll get him dead. But my way."

He rose and headed for the door. From behind him Jupiter said, disbelief in his tone, "Where do you think you're going?"

"To meet him."

"Never."

He turned very slowly, very dangerously, like lightning capable of leaping from the bottle at any second. "You going to stop me, Jupe? We been together a long time. You going to try to stop me?"

"They'll blow your head off the moment you step out the door."

"No. He's like me. We're going to do this, and everybody who needs to know, knows it."

He started for the door and suddenly Jupiter shouted loud enough to be heard outside, "You expect me to send one of my people out?'' Shai stopped and turned, puzzled, and Jupiter continued, ''If you're who I think you are . . . you step out first. Of course . . . we have guns, too. We might just decide to shoot you.''

There was a dead silence. Jupiter smiled in the dimness and said, ''See?''

But Shai was peering through a small hole in the door, and now he looked around. ''He's coming out into the open.''

''Shoot him. This time do it right.''

Slowly Shai shook his head. ''Got to be this way. And sad part is, you'd never understand why.'' And with that he walked out of the cabin.

Winkowski saw him emerge and brought his gun up, ready to shoot. ''Give the word, Sergeant,'' he said hoarsely.

She watched as a tall, muscled black man walked away from the cabin in slow, measured steps. Walking in the other direction was Chuck, arms loose and relaxed, the dog at his side . . .

''Son of a bitch,'' she whispered.

''What?'' said Winkowski, his gaze riveted on the black man. Then he followed where she was looking and he saw it, too.

Chuck was wearing a blindfold.

The black man had stopped, and he was looking surprised as well. ''What's this for?'' he asked.

''Wouldn't want to make it too easy for me,'' said Chuck calmly.

''I'm not fighting you like that.''

''You afraid?''

''It's not honorable.''

''You are afraid. Afraid that I'll beat you, even like this,'' said Chuck.

''You can't possibly.''

''If I do, you let the girl go.''

"You won't beat me that way," said the black man with finality.

"In that case," said Chuck, "you have nothing to lose."

The black man was silent for a moment. "All right," he said.

Rommel seemed to drift away slightly as Chuck fell into a natural defensive pose. The black man struck a stance as well, standing in a t-form like a fencer, his weight balanced on his back leg.

"Let me plug that bastard," said Winkowski tersely.

"Hold off," she said.

At that moment her comm unit squawked. She picked it up and said, "Panther Six here."

"Panther One-one," came the brisk voice. "There's been a change of plan. Word from high command is to bomb the Extremists and have done with it."

Her eyes widened. "What?"

"Bombing begins in five minutes. We will be using high-localizers and limited impact, but I would nevertheless suggest you leave the area."

"You can't! There's hostages . . ."

"Too bad."

"An agent with the Complex."

"I don't care if the Chief of Staff is in there," said Sutphin, "our policy for terrorists is no deals, no negotiation. Extermination. Squash them. S.O.P. You know that. Five minutes. Panther One-one out."

She stared at the comm unit a moment longer. "Winkowski," she said quietly, "evacuate."

"But, Sergeant . . ."

"Now," she said sharply and, seeing the impact it had on him, added a bit more softly, "move your ass, Winkowski. I'll see you in a bit."

Biting back a reply, he moved away from her, vanishing into the woods. And she added under her breath, "Or maybe you'll see me in bits."

25

"YOUR DOG GOING to jump in for you if things get tough?" said Shai, not moving from his position.

"He's giving me hints," Chuck replied.

"Oh. Right," said Shai.

He's still moving, Rommel said. *There's nothing in between the two of you. You can move to your left or right and— look out, here he comes.*

Chuck had been alerted. He'd heard the scuffling of feet, sensed the sudden shift in the air.

Shai came in quickly. Chuck listened to every movement, tried to feel the direction, listened to Rommel's coaching, and his arm lashed out to block. But Shai suddenly spun and came in with a reverse snap kick that landed hard and fierce in Chuck's stomach. Chuck went down to one knee, gasping.

He kicked you in the stomach, Rommel told him helpfully.

"Thanks," gasped out Chuck.

Shai was back in position, fists clenched. shaking his head. "This is pointless," he said.

"You're . . . afraid," said Chuck, staggering to his feet.

Thin-lipped, Shai came in fast again.

He's going to piss on you, Rommel said.

It took a split second for Chuck to mentally translate that to mean that Shai was about to launch a side snap kick, because to Rommel, that's what it would look like. He heard the scuffle of the foot on dirt, sensed the sudden shift, and pivoted, just feeling the leg whistle by. He grabbed it, carrying the weight through, and momentarily immobilized Shai. Chuck twisted, his leg lashing out, and he knocked Shai completely off his feet, slamming him face first into the dirt.

Shai shook loose from the grip and rolled away, getting to his feet more cautiously this time.

Nice job, said Rommel.

''Thanks again,'' said Chuck.

At that moment he heard a fierce barking and realized that it wasn't Rommel.

The Dobie, the one called Mars, had sensed Rommel's nearness and leaped through the window, charging at Rommel. His jaws snapped furiously as he leaped at the German shepherd.

''Rommel!'' shouted Chuck, horrified. The sounds of the two dogs going at each other was a hideous one, snapping and pure savagery and movement—

Movement—

Shai was moving and Chuck tried to react, but he was distracted and a fierce punch slammed into the side of his head. He fell and rolled, trying to put some distance between them, and he clambered to his feet. He was disoriented, lost, paying attention not to his battle but to the death struggle of Rommel.

Another kick to the side and he went down, clutching. He heard Shai's breathing as the big man came after him, heard his feet as he shifted quickly. It had all gone wrong, Rommel was supposed to guide him, help him . . . but Rommel was fighting to survive, was fighting with his guts and his instinct . . . Movement, where? There . . .

He didn't know what it was he was blocking, but his arm swept up, brushing aside the strike of the foot. And now he had the ankle. Ankles could be turned, and twisted, and broken.

Tae Kwan Do was what Shai was using. Karate discipline, primarily with legs. Aikido could take it. Dammit, it *could*.

He twisted, feeling the ankle creak under his grip. From the darkness Shai cried out, and into the darkness Shai's body fell.

Chuck was on his knees and from the darkness he sensed Shai's lunge. Shai was on his knees as well. *Suwari-waza*, kneeling techniques. Lord knew they were fresh on Chuck's mind—he'd just done the *shikko* across who knew how much forest land.

He caught Shai's hard-edged slash on the edge of his forearm, deflecting the strength of the blow and depleting it, and then grabbed Shai's wrist and twisted. Shai's entire arm bent backward and Shai slammed to the ground once again.

From his twisted position Shai struck back. Even though the movement caused pain to rip through his entire shoulder, Shai managed to get his leg between himself and Chuck and shove out against Chuck's chest. Chuck's grip wasn't as sure as it could have been and he lost it, Shai tearing away from him.

They both got to their feet.

Chuck's heart was beating double time. He slowed it down, reached into himself. Heard the beating, heard the pulse of his forehead. He screened out the snarling sounds of the dogs—it couldn't be part of his world now. He sank down, down into the inner calm of his being. And yes, there was his heart, now beating more calmly and certainly.

There was the sound of his breathing.

There was the sound of Shai's breathing, as certain as his own. His mind focused, bringing himself into tune with Shai. He heard and felt the movement of Shai's feet, knew where Shai's arms would be, sensed where the hands would be. He knew Shai as he knew himself, and in his mind there was the outline of his opponent. As surely as if he were seeing him with his own eyes. Better . . . because eyes could be deceived. But the mind's eye knew the moves that Shai would make, planned the blocks and knew the counterstrikes.

Jo glanced at her watch. She looked to the skies. Nothing yet. But within moments . . .

Shai came in quickly. Chuck backed up slightly, to diffuse the momentum, and Shai attacked with a dazzling array of kicks and strikes. He screamed repeatedly, his *"Ki Ya"* filling the air, and Chuck paid them no mind. He was a blur, blocking every thrust, turning away every strike, creating a wall of muscle and bone that Shai could not penetrate.

Shai slammed forward with a punch and Chuck caught the arm. He twisted at the waist, full strength, hard and fast as Shai went past him, and there was a snap that was audible throughout the area. Shai went down, screaming, clutching at the broken arm, and he staggered to his feet.

Chuck stood there, poised, relaxed, clothes torn and body covered with dirt and grime.

"It's over," he said quietly.

Shai paused, gasping. Then slowly he screened out the throbbing pain that was in his shattered left arm, and he nodded. "Yes," he said, as much to himself as to Chuck, "at long last, it is."

Suddenly Chuck realized the snarling had stopped. "Rommel!" he said urgently. Dead silence. "Rommel!" he said again.

From nearby there was a rustling of bushes and then a voice said, *Nice of you to care.*

He knelt down as Rommel came to him, and he ran his fingers across the great dog's fur. It was torn and bloodied, and Rommel's breath was coming quickly, like a steam engine. "Where's the other dog?"

And from nearby Shai said, "He's dead."

Chuck turned slowly in the direction of the voice. Rommel said in his mind, *He's right. I had no choice. Him or me.*

"I'm sorry," Chuck said softly.

Shai said nothing, which was his habit when he had nothing to say.

Moments later Shai entered the cabin. Jupiter took a step forward as Shai leaned against the wall.

"My God," whispered Jupiter.

But Shai wasn't paying attention. Instead he was gesturing to Dakota. "Go," he whispered hoarsely. He pointed at Luta, adding, "And take her with you."

Dakota started to get to her feet, pulling the bleeding Luta up, and then she saw the gun in Jupiter's hand. "She's not going anywhere," said Jupiter.

"I gave my word," said Shai, and that was when Jupiter saw the gun in Shai's hand.

"I didn't give mine."

"I don't care. You shoot them, Jupe, I'll shoot you. You really ready to admit you won't get out alive? Really ready to say that to yourself? Are you?"

Jupiter didn't speak. His gun didn't move. He might have been an alabaster statue.

"Go," said Shai softly. "Go now."

The women moved, and Jupiter's gun moved with them. It tracked them slowly across the room and came to rest on Shai as they went past him. Shai aimed at Jupiter, Jupiter at Shai. From Jupiter there projected an aura of desperation and from Shai, quiet determination.

Dakota kept moving, limping terribly, pulling Luta along as best she could. And Shai and Jupiter did not move, still aiming, a silent struggle of wills being fought.

Dakota glanced over her shoulder and then pulled open the door, shouting, "I'm coming out! I'm coming out! It's me!"

"No," said Jupiter from behind her. From the sound of his voice it was clear that he had completely lost touch with reality. "She's mine. She stays." But there wasn't even a sense in it that he thought she was going to, and Dakota quickly yanked Luta through the door.

* * *

Jo broke from cover, running toward the two women as they half staggered, half fell from the cabin. Chuck was moving too, a hand on Rommel's back as they ran toward Dakota.

"Chuck!" cried out Dakota, and a few yards from the cabin the two of them collapsed.

"We've gotta get away from here, fast," said Jo, running to them.

"Oh, but it's like home," Dakota said sarcastically.

"I mean it, you—" And Jo suddenly looked up, her ears already telling her what her eyes were confirming. "Let's go!" she shouted. "Let's go, let's go, *let's go!*"

And she pushed and yanked and shoved, and the four of them ran and staggered from the cabin as the choppers dove down toward the hideout of the Extremists.

Inside, Shai and Jupiter still held their guns on each other.

"We fought well," said Shai softly. "And now we'll die well. And I'll be with my family."

"You don't understand," said Jupiter. "We're going to get away."

"Are we?" asked Shai. A touch of amusement reached his eyes.

"Oh, yes," said Jupiter, his eyes glazing. "You see . . . I've got a plan." And he proceeded to explain it.

Shai had trouble hearing the details because of the sharp whistling sound from overhead. Jupiter was oblivious to it, of course, and he was still outlining the details of his plan when the bomb hit.

26

"HE'S A PSIONIC, all right," Major Sutphin told her. "But he doesn't work for the Complex. He's on the run *from* the Complex."

Jo stood opposite Sutphin across his desk, and she was not entirely able to hide the astonishment she felt. When she, along with the survivors of their nice routine overnight, had arrived back at Fort Morris, she had thought her troubles over. Now they were just beginning.

Sutphin tapped the computer screen on his desk. There was a CONFIDENTIAL flasher on the upper right, and on the upper left was Chuck's name.

"He's extremely dangerous," said Sutphin. "A rogue assassin. We are to keep him heavily sedated until they can send people here to apprehend him. Some guy named Beutel is assigned to the case."

"Beutel." She rolled the name over in her mind. *Tell Butte . . . Beutel.* "Yeah. Okay."

"Yeah okay?" said Sutphin. "Sergeant, head over to the base hospital immediately. That is where they're being kept? He and the woman, plus that other Extremist we captured?"

"Yes, sir."

"Good. Move your keister." He was picking up the phone. "I'm going to warn them he's to be kept sedated. You get over there and supervise it . . . and then start pumping the woman for information.''

She saluted stiffly, and then said, ''Sir, with all due respect, he doesn't seem like the type who would be—''

''I don't recall asking your opinion, Sergeant,'' he said, his moustache bristling.

''No, sir. Thank you, sir.'' She turned on her heel and left.

Dakota looked up from her hospital bed to see Chuck looking in at her. Her eyes widened in surprise . . . primarily because she was looking into his.

''You're okay!'' she gasped. It had been barely hours since they had been brought there, and during that time she had agonized over how (she was certain) Chuck's life was going to be living hell, going through it in darkness.

He walked forward and embraced her. ''Still a little light sensitive,'' he admitted, ''but I've got most of it back. My power helps me to heal somehow.''

''Power of positive thinking, probably.''

''Maybe,'' he said. ''I don't know. We'll have a chance to discuss it later. Come on—''

''No.''

The answer surprised him. ''What?''

She smiled and took his chin in her hands. ''First, with all my injuries, I'd only slow you down. I don't have the power you do. Second . . . I think I've had it with running around. Maybe I'll go back to the circus. Or maybe I'll go back and mend some old family fences, which is just like tightrope walking, only more dangerous. No matter what, I think you've kind of worn me out, Chuck.''

''I'm—I'm sorry . . .''

''Don't be. It was a trip. C'mon . . . first you tried to talk me out of coming with you, and now you don't want me to leave. Men. So fickle.'' She drew her face to him and kissed him once on either cheek, and then for a long, lingering moment on the lips. She let him go and smiled. "I love you, Chuck. Don't be a stranger . . . wherever I am. Okay?"

"Okay."

He moved away from her and into the hallway. Rommel was waiting there next to the two guards Chuck had already rendered unconscious. *She's not coming?*

"No."

Bitches. What did you expect?

"I expected exactly what she said. Come on."

They moved down the hallway and as they passed a room, a female voice said, "Hey . . . you . . ."

Chuck turned and saw Luta lying there, haggard, drawn and pale, hooked up to tubes and monitors.

"You're a psi, aren't you," she said. It was not a question. He nodded.

"There's more of us," she said, very softly, very hoarsely. "More than you would think. More going there, every day. When there's enough . . . there's going to be a revolution . . . they could use you . . ."

"Where?" said Chuck urgently. "Go where?"

"I don't know. Heard about it . . . rumors . . . talk . . ."

"What did you hear?"

And she whispered one word before her strength left her and she slipped back into a deep sleep. And the word was . . . *"Haven."*

Jo sped in a Jeep toward the base hospital, her mind racing. She thought over everything that had happened, tried to reconcile what she had seen with what she had been told.

She loved the army, embraced the army. She loved the rules, the order, and the regulation.

Assassin. The ugly word rolled across her mind.

And then she spotted him, moving across the base, sticking to the shadows of a storage building. Him and his dog, an unmistakable pair.

She turned the wheel sharply and barreled toward them, pulling her gun from her holster.

Chuck looked up and saw her. His arms rested at his sides and he made no move. Rommel growled warningly and Chuck muttered a word to Rommel to get him to stay.

The Jeep screeched up to them and slammed to a halt. Jo Sanderson sat up on the top of her seat, her gun aimed at him.

They said nothing for a long moment. She stepped out of the jeep, keeping the gun leveled on him.

"I saved your life," he said quietly.

"I saved yours," she replied.

He stared at her for a long moment. "You're one of us," he said.

She looked at him oddly. "What?"

"Like us. Like me. When one of us is around the other, we just—just know. I know. You're like me. You must know it by now."

She remembered—remembered hearing the scream of agony when the factory went up . . . the scream that no one could hear . . .

"No, I'm not," she said firmly.

They said nothing.

"I won't do anything against you," said Chuck. "Arrest me. Do what you have to."

What're you, nuts?

"Shut up, Rommel."

She looked from one to the other. "You talk to the dog."

"Of course."

"Of course." She shrugged.

She held out her gun and reversed it, proffering the butt end to him. "Take it."

"What?"

"And the Jeep. Get the hell out of here. There's guards at the front gate, but that shouldn't slow you and Rin-Tin-Tin down. You heard me. Get out. Oh . . . but hit me first." She turned, presenting the back of her skull. "I have an image to protect."

"I can't hit you."

"Then my ass is grass for letting you walk out. Hit me."

She braced herself and the impact came, sending her to the ground.

She lay there, hugging the pavement, and listened as the Jeep started up and roared off. Then she raised her head and watched him go, the large dog hunkering down in the back.

Jo reached around and touched the back of her head gently. Not even enough for a lump. He hadn't even been fierce enough to give her a goddamn lump.

Shaking her head, she stood, placed her back against the brick wall of the small building, then brought her head forward and then back as hard as she could, slamming it into the wall. Stars exploded behind her eyes as she sank to the ground.

Some assassin, she thought, and passed out.